At Half-Light

At Half-Light

A Story of Tango and Memory

Linda Walsh

KENTON
ROAD
PRESS

Toronto

Published by Kenton Road Press
Toronto, Canada
www.kentonroadpress.ca

Cover design by Kristy Hill,
Umbrella Squared Design Group
Cover painting by Linda Walsh
Photographs by Linda Walsh & Oscar Casas

Excerpts of lyrics from the tangos
"El Día Que Me Quieras" (Alfredo Le
Pera, 1935), "Por una Cabeza" (Alfredo Le
Pera, 1935), "La Morocha" (Ángel Villoldo,
1905), "El Choclo" (Ángel Villoldo, 1903),
and "Volver" (Alfredo Le Pera, 1934)
are in the public domain.

Grateful acknowledgement to Oscar Casas
for permission to reprint excerpts from
the tango "Flaco, Fino, y Delicado."
Copyright © 1990 by Oscar Casas.

ISBN 978-1-7782877-2-5

For my parents,
Daniel and Jo,
who filled our house with books.

And for Oscar Casas and his parents,
Oscar and Mafalda,
who gave me the tango.

CONTENTS

RESIDENTS OF THE HOUSE IN BUENOS AIRES

Armando Rodríguez, younger brother of Esteban.

Dolores, mother of Gloria, aunt of La Renga.

El Ciego, son of Esteban Rodríguez and Gloria. Also called Esteban.

El Dentista, also called Héctor.

El Loco, name unknown.

El Perro, the dog.

Esteban Rodríguez, older brother of Armando, father of El Ciego. Also called El Señor.

Gloria, daughter of Dolores, mother of El Ciego.

La Chica, prostitute working for El Puño, name unknown.

La Niña Bonita, also called La Bonita or Laura.

La Renga, also called Pepita, Doña Pepa, or Josefa.

La Rusa, mother of Iva and Marek. Also called Marina.

Los Gallegos – Juan (father), Manuel (son), and Manuel's two little brothers, names unknown.

Los Palitos, two skinny brothers, names unknown.

Tito, also called Alberto Torres and (by his granddaughter, Ale) Lito.

∞

The infinity sign,
indicating time movements in the story,
represents the *ocho,*
the figure eight,
a dance element in Argentine tango.

AT HALF-LIGHT

Sunday evening in Buenos Aires, 1936. You stroll through the crowd along Corrientes Street, carried by the human tide towards the moon behind the Obelisk. In balconies hang baskets of malvón, *the flowers red as burning coals. At number 348, you push the door open and take the elevator to the second floor. The night slides open. Inside, where it's always evening, you breathe in the heady mix of comfort and danger. Voices – in Italian, Portuguese, Spanish, and other languages you don't recognize. The* porteño* *words for woman – not* mujer, *but* mina, pebeta, percanta *– with no rolling consonants to soften their edges. Black lacquer and burgundy, a fringed lamp on a table draped with velvet, a piano, and from the phonograph, the wail of the* bandoneón.†

Dark eyes behind a fan lowered just enough to catch the flicker of eyelashes, the flush on a cheek, the promise of a promise. You've gone back night after night for a glimpse of her – this

---

* a person from the city of Buenos Aires
† a type of concertina, a typical instrument in most tango ensembles

5

woman who will be my grandmother. For you, she has no name yet, no address, no family. You do not yet imagine the small room where the dress she's wearing will later hang from the back of a chair under the window that looks out onto Balcarce Street. She is still only music and half-light.

You tell me about the Río de la Plata, the River of Silver. "It's not like this little Canadian river. It's so wide that you can't see the other side, One day, mi amor, *I'm gonna take you there."*

But I don't want to hear about rivers. I want more stories about Sunday evenings in Buenos Aires, more stories about my grandmother and the tango – pictures that have been woven into my imagination.

I persist until you conjure more images that work their way into my dreams, just as the music had seeped through the cracks of sorrow and oppression in the walls of the conventillos, *the tenement houses full of people who had left their countries and taken the long journey to Argentina, looking for a dream. El tango – music born of pain, desire, and longing for what had been left behind.*

∞

My grandfather's name is Alberto Torres. I call him Lito, short for *abuelito.*[*] Everyone else calls him Tito. He came to Canada to live with us when I was two, and I spent a lot of time with him because my parents both

---

[*] diminutive of *abuelo*, grandfather

taught at the university. I sometimes felt as if I were living in two places – my parents' house beside the little river in Peterborough and the big house in Lito's stories, the one with the tango patio in Buenos Aires near the Río de la Plata, a river the colour of *dulce de leche* and so wide you can't see the other side. I would close my eyes and imagine myself in the Café Tortoni on the Avenida de Mayo, amid the ghosts of the tango singer Carlos Gardel and the poets Alfonsina and Borges, the tango sweetened by Argentinian pastries with magical names – *masas finas, alfajores. Medialuna* – the half-moon on my tongue.

I was fascinated by magic as a kid. It started when I saw *Doug Henning's World of Magic* on TV when I was five. I loved Henning's satin suits covered in stars, his silver boots, and his magical house with the rooms of the present, the past, and the future. He could pull reflections of candles from mirrors, saw girls in half and put them back together again, and make handkerchiefs dance and glasses of chocolate milk appear. He made people disappear and reappear inside boxes with red curtains. At the end of the show, he said that nothing was impossible. You just had to look inside.

Lito gave me a magic set for Christmas – a box with a secret drawer, some rings that passed through one another if you hit them at just the right angle, two red silk scarves, a shiny gold cape, a wand, and a magician's hat with a big silver star on the front. I would practice for hours and put on magic shows for my parents and Lito.

One evening, as I was helping my father set the table for dinner, we talked about my day at school and, of course, about magic.

"I've been working on some card tricks that Lito showed me, Papá."

"Oh? Great! You can show me after dinner."

"I want to be a magician when I grow up."

"Well, keep practicing."

"I want to be as good as Doug Henning. He can make birds and cards and even people disappear, and then he makes them appear again. I want to learn how to do that. How does he do it? Where do people go when they disappear?"

My mother had her back to us, stirring the pasta sauce on the stove. Suddenly, the spoon clattered on the tile floor. As she bent down to pick it up, I could see her shoulders shaking, as if something cold and dark were passing through her. My father looked over at her and then at me. Still with her back to us, my mother turned on the tap, rinsed the spoon, ripped off a piece of paper towel, and wiped the spoon and then her face with it.

"I'm not sure, Ale.* One day, maybe we'll find the

---

* short form of Alejandra, pronounced **Ah-**lay

answer," My father stood up. "Now, please go and call Lito for dinner. I'll help Mami bring the food to the table." He put his hands on my mother's shoulders and kissed her cheek. I ran down to the river to find Lito.

We didn't talk about magic during dinner that night. My mother was trying her best not to let me see she'd been crying, but I could tell anyway and it frightened me. Had some magician put my grandmother in a disappearing box and forgotten how to bring her back? Maybe that was the reason she wasn't here. Later, in my room, instead of doing my homework, I wrote a letter to Doug Henning, asking him how to undisappear people. I stopped asking questions and started putting together pieces of the stories of Argentina and where my grandmother was, in my own way.

One afternoon, I was looking at pictures in one of my mother's *National Geographic* magazines. Inside, I found a note from the school about my "somewhat disturbing" stories and drawings.

A few days later, when my mother came to pick me up after school, she said we were going to see my teacher and the principal.

"Have I done something wrong, Mami?"

No, *mi amor*." My mother took my hand and squeezed it. "You haven't done anything wrong at all. They just want to talk to us."

We walked in silence along the hall towards the

principal's office, past the bulletin boards with student artwork. Pinned to the one from our class were pictures of flowers, trees, cars, cats, dogs, kids swimming, rainbows. I'd checked the board every day, waiting for my drawings to be up there with the others. When the door opened into the principal's office, I saw mine. There. On his desk.

My teacher and the principal smiled together, first at my mother and then at me, and asked us to sit down. The principal sat in his big chair on the other side of his desk and my teacher sat in the chair beside me.

"Who is the girl in this one, Alejandra? Is it you?" The teacher pointed to my drawing of a girl in a disappearing box in Doug Henning's room of the past.

"No."

"Who is she?"

"The magician's assistant."

"Why is she in a box?"

"Because the magician's gonna make her disappear. It's a disappearing box."

"Is she afraid?"

"I don't think so. She knows he'll make her appear again."

"She likes magic shows," my mother offered.

"And this one? Who is she? Is she the same girl?" My teacher pointed to the one of a girl sawn in half, with her feet sticking out of the side of one box and her head poking out of another.

"No, she's the magician's other assistant."

"Where's the magician?"

"In another picture." I had that one at home. The magician was dressed like Doug Henning. I'd stuck silver stars onto his black hat.

"Why is she cut in half?"

"That's what magicians do." I was getting impatient. It was obvious the teacher and the principal knew nothing about magic. I felt like grabbing my drawings off the desk and walking out. "But she'll get put back together again. It doesn't hurt." I hoped that would make them feel better and they'd let us leave.

After answering a few more questions, I had to wait out in the hall while they talked to my mother for what felt like forever. I just wanted to get out of there. Lito had promised to show me some more card tricks after school, and that was all I could think about.

To pass the time while I was waiting, I walked back along the hall and had another look at our board with the pictures – Sarah's rainbows, Matthew's bicycles. Becky's red cars, Caroline's flowers, Eric's sunny day. No magic.

When my mother finally came out of the office, I could tell she was upset. "Let's go, Ale. This meeting is finished." We didn't talk in the car on the way home.

Later, Lito and I sat on the floor at the coffee table in the living room. He shuffled the special cards and spread them out. I was ready for more magic. I told him where we'd been that afternoon and the questions they'd asked me about my drawings, and I asked him what "somewhat disturbing" meant.

After dinner that evening, I was up in my room finishing my homework and Lito and my parents were talking in Spanish in the kitchen. I couldn't make out most of what my parents were saying, but I could certainly hear Lito. That was the only time I ever remember him raising his voice.

"Those teachers are fools. Tell them to leave Ale alone. What do they know, those *pelotudos,** living in this country where the only dangerous thing is the food? What do they know about anything? They are all stupid, fat, and crazy."

When he put on one of his tango records and started singing along with Alberto Castillo to "Así se Baila el Tango,"† I knew it was safe to go downstairs.

"Ale, come in! Time to dance! Ah, Castillo. What a voice! Just listen to that!" Lito sang as loud as he could. "He was a doctor, you know, not only a tango singer. They say there was always a lineup of ladies at his office door."

My mother cut him off with one of her famous looks. "Papá! *Por favor*! Enough."

Lito turned up the music, singing with Dr. Castillo. "Remember, Ale, you are *porteña,* a girl from Buenos

---

* jerks
† That's how you dance tango.

Aires, and you must dance like one, walk like one. Tall and proud. *Ahora sí.* Yes, that's it! Nothing better than dancing with you!"

I don't know what they did with my drawings, but I didn't care. I just drew more. I never told them that the girl in the disappearing box was my grandmother. If they'd looked carefully, they would have easily known it was her. The soft dark hair, the orange dress. I wasn't sure who the other girl was – the one sawn in half.

My dreams were filled with the people and places in Lito's stories. A man wearing a black hat covered in stars flew through the night sky. A blind man danced with a dog and horses rode bicycles. A pretty girl whispered secrets across a shining river. But sometimes there was no music or stars or dancing animals or pretty girls, and the secrets scared me. I dreamed one night of a box floating on the surface of a great, dark, silent river under a black, starless sky. The box opened and I could see my grandmother's face. When the box sank and disappeared, I woke up terrified, sweating. I couldn't sleep, so I crept downstairs to the kitchen. Lito was sitting at the table, drinking *mate.*[*]

"*Che,*[†] *mi amor,* you can't sleep either? *Vení.*" He pulled a chair close to his and patted the seat. "Not all dreams have happy endings, and I know that can make

---

[*] Traditional South American tea. Also the name of the container from which it is drunk. Pronounced **ma**-*tay*.
[†] Hey

it difficult to sleep. Come here and we will drink some *mate*." For me, he always added sugar. "But be very quiet. If your mother finds out that I give you *mate* at this time of night, she's gonna kill me.

"You know, Ale, your *abuelita*, she was the prettiest girl in Buenos Aires. Look." He took out the picture of my grandmother that he always carried in his shirt pocket. It had been taken in a park in Buenos Aires on a summer day.

"The first time we went out together, we went to the Cine Porteño. I used to work there selling tickets three nights a week and I got free ones sometimes. I remember when they showed the film *Melodía de Arrabal* with Carlos Gardel. When Carlitos sang 'Silencio' in that movie, everyone went crazy, clapping and yelling for that part to be played again. They did the same when he sang 'Melodía de Arrabal.' Imagine! They had to wind the movie back." Lito threw his arms into the air and rotated them backwards, pretending to nearly fall off his chair. It always made me laugh when he did stuff like that.

"Your *abuelita* had soft, soft hair, dark like you. And her dancing! Was like dancing with an angel. Like magic. When we went to the *milongas*,* everyone wanted to dance with her, but she only danced with me. She said that, after me, was never gonna be the same with anyone else. And I never wanted to dance with another

---

* tango dance venues

14

girl. Until you, of course." He gently ran his hand over the top of my head.

"The first time that I saw your *abuelita* was on Balcarce Street. She was buying carrots. She was perfect! Her voice, her smile, the way that her skirt moved when she turned. I could understand in that moment exactly how El Dentista felt when he saw Claudia. I have no choice. I have to talk to her, but I'm afraid she's gonna laugh at me. I have an idea – buy some carrots! Only twenty centavos in my pocket and I'm buying carrots! But she smiled at me, *mi amor*, so was all worth it. She lived with her aunt. Well, not really an aunt, but…well, anyway, she lived with her aunt.

"One night, Manuel takes me to a building on Corrientes Street, where he says that there are pretty girls who might dance with you. We go up to the second floor in a shaky elevator like a big bird cage. We knock, the door opens, and inside is music and people dancing. After one drink, I see her – the girl who I saw buying the carrots. She looks different – that orange dress, high heels, the soft hair tied back. But the smile, ah, *mi amor*, that was the same. I was completely in love!"

I drifted on his voice as he carried me upstairs and put me back into bed. I had another dream that night of my grandmother in an orange dress dancing along a silver river.

Years later, when he said I was old enough to know,

he told me my grandmother's "aunt" was actually a *puta,* a prostitute, and if he hadn't met my grandmother, she might have ended up a *puta* too.

"Your *abuelita*'s parents died when she was very young, jus' like mine did. The lady that she called her aunt was a good woman. She took care of her, jus' the way that Doña Pepa took care of me. They were very poor, and sometimes poor people have to do things that rich people do not."

∞

These days, Lito doesn't do much except sit outside and stare at the river, drinking *mate,* lost in time. His memories and all the stories he told me when I was growing up – about the people in the house in Buenos Aires, the tango, and my grandmother – are unravelling bit by bit. When I need to pull him back to me, I grab the cassette player and a couple of tango tapes and go out and sit with him.

"El Dentista. Remember him, Lito? He taught Juan and Esteban to ride the bike around the patio?" I push the play button. Carlos Gardel is halfway through singing "Por una Cabeza,"[*] a tango about risking everything on the horses and love and losing it all.

"They all used to tell me their stories. El Dentista almost died, you know. For the love of a woman who

---

[*] By a Head

never knew him," Lito says.

"Claudia." I've heard this story many times.

"Yes, that was her name. How did you know that?"

"You told me, Lito, a long time ago. And El Dentista lost all El Chino's money on the horses, so El Chino's men beat him up. He almost died, but he was tough."

My grandfather smiles, the music leading him back. He picks up the thermos and adds hot water to the *mate*. "Yes, Juan and Esteban brought him some of Doña Pepa's soup. That's all El Dentista could eat with the broken jaw. He was crazy for that girl Claudia, you know."

"Just the way Esteban was for La Chica, right? Both of them crazy for girls they could never have."

"Yes, Esteban never even knew that poor girl's name. No one did. Everyone just called her La Chica – the girl – even us kids." He shakes his head slowly.

I change the cassette. Donato's orchestra plays "Te Busco." I'm looking for you.

"Ah, Donato! *Bailamos,* Ale?" He takes my hand gently and I help him stand up. I wait for him to say what he always does. "Don't think. Jus' follow me. Listen to the music and your feet will move by themselves."

I close my eyes and we're dancing just as we always have. But when the music stops, he slips from my embrace and turns back towards the river. Every time this happens, I feel we're both disappearing. I lead him back to his chair and kiss his cheek. I take him by the shoulders and look straight into his face.

"Lito, *te busco*." But I've lost him again. "I promise I'll remember them, Lito – La Niña Bonita, Gloria, Dolores, El Loco, Doña Pepa, La Chica, La Rusa, Esteban, El Dentista. All of them. Even that miserable Armando and the thug, El Puño."

My grandfather stares at the river, and I begin to write.

LA RENGA

"Doña Pepa was kind of the boss of the house," Lito said. "She was like a mother to me. We sometimes sat together on the patio when she wasn't sweeping and cleaning and she told me stories about my mother and the other people in the house. She said that I had a good memory and she was telling me the stories so that there will be someone to remember them. She had a bad leg and couldn't walk very well, so they called her La Renga. Not a nice name to call anyone, but in Argentina in those days, and now too, there were lots of nicknames. Some were not so nice. Of course, we kids didn't call her that. We had to be more polite, so we called her Doña Pepa. She walked like this." Lito took a few steps, throwing his right leg out to the side in a circular motion, sending his body forward as it landed. "She always had a long skirt, so it looked like she was doing a little jump. When I was a kid, I jus' thought she was dancing all the time."

∞

La Renga stabbed her broom at the ground under the

chairs on the patio. "Stupid pieces of shit, sons of whores, no better than garbage!" She made sure her curses could be heard all the way up to the second floor. The dog limped after her as she dug out cigarette butts from the corners. It sniffed at the broom, narrowly missing a crack on the head with it, and scratched its ragged ear with a hind foot.

"All those good-for-nothing pieces of crap! They keep me awake all night with that infernal noise, drinking and whoring until the sun comes up, rubbing their bodies against one another. They call that dancing!" La Renga spat at the ground.

"Smoking, drinking, fornicating like cats, like the sons of whores they are! And then I have to clean up after them. Not like the days when Señor Rodríguez and his family lived here, when this was a decent house and those louts and their *putas* were out in the streets, where they belonged."

The dog scratched under the sink, found a dried-up piece of meat, and dodged the broom again.

"And you too, Perro, you useless dog, only after food. I should throw you back out in the street, where you came from. This house has too many strays." She'd rescued the dog from a gang of boys armed with stones. It had taken cover in the doorway, and the shouts and steady thud of stones against the door brought her out. The boys scattered when they saw her. One of the dog's hind legs was bleeding. She gave it some scraps of meat and a bowl of water, and it kept coming back, waiting at the door for food until, one day, she let it in.

Sweeping was the only thing that calmed her nerves, and since it was done in full view of everyone in the house, it was a way to let all of them know how much work those worthless *cabrones** gave her every day.

Sweeping had been her first job when she arrived there almost fifty years before. At nine years of age, she limped behind her mother through the streets to this house, where her mother's sister Dolores worked for the Rodríguez family. They knocked and waited for the big door to open. Tía Dolores appeared and hurried them in, telling them to be quiet, giving them a black look that could only be responded to with silence – the kind of silence that meant more than not saying anything. It meant silence from the top of your head right down to your toes. Pepita prayed that her leg would obey the order. Summoning all her concentration, she willed it to behave, not to slap the ground when she walked. No *milonga,* no nonsense.

Pepita had never seen such a big house. In the central patio, which was open to the sky, there was a tall tree. On three sides of the patio, there were doors to many rooms. A stairway led up to the second floor, where there were corridors with doors to more rooms.

---

* bastards

"I'm going now, Pepita," her mother said. "You will stay with Tía Dolores." She kissed her daughter and didn't look back. The heavy door clanged shut behind her and she was gone. Pepita was left alone with her mother's sister, who had always frightened her. Tía Dolores was thin and wiry and always wore the same black dress and stockings. She looked like a little black bird that might peck your eyes out if you weren't careful.

"Come with me, Josefa." Tía Dolores was the only one who ever called her Josefa. Pepita followed her aunt, listening to what she could and couldn't do, what she should and shouldn't say, to whom she should and shouldn't speak, at whom and at what she should and shouldn't look. On no account was she to enter any of the rooms except the kitchen and the room she slept in. She was to do exactly what Tía Dolores said, exactly when she was told to do it.

Dolores handed her a broom. "One of your jobs will be to sweep the patio and the stairs. You can start now. Don't leave a speck of dirt or you'll get no lunch and maybe no dinner."

Pepita shared a room with Dolores' daughter, Gloria, a thin, sullen girl of sixteen, who liked to order her about and tell her lurid stories about the things she did with Señor Rodríguez when his wife wasn't watching.

"I swear I'll break that other leg of yours, Renga, if

you tell anyone about it."

Pepita saw them one morning. Señor Rodríguez' hand on Gloria's behind, just for a few seconds as he passed her in the corridor upstairs. She was sure this was one of the things she shouldn't see. She concentrated on her broom and swept harder. Sometimes when Señora Rodríguez was out shopping with her sister, Pepita could hear Gloria and Señor Rodríguez in the library. Gloria had told her he had a bed in there, where he slept when his wife wanted to be alone.

"They had a baby that died, a boy. He got some kind of fever. Since then, El Señor sleeps in the library a lot. The sheets on that bed are so soft, Renga, just like silk. I feel like a princess when I touch them."

Imagining those silken sheets against Gloria's skin made Pepita sweep hard. Thinking of her mother, whose face was getting harder and harder to remember, made the broom move even faster. If she thought of the people who looked at her leg and whispered, it was as if the broom moved by itself. She would sweep until she had swept them all away, swept away even the name her mother had given her. She was no longer Josefa or Pepita. She was called La Renga. Just a girl who swept.

La Renga, the cripple. El Ciego, the blind man. The names that our mothers gave us are forgotten, buried, and mean nothing now.

Esteban, that poor blind devil in the room upstairs, wasn't supposed to have been born at all. And now he's gone and fallen in love with that girl who belongs to the guy they call the fist – El Puño. It's all my fault for putting her in the room beside Esteban's, but what could I do? Send the girl back out into the street? At least in here she only has one thug to deal with. She didn't look more than fifteen when El Puño brought her here. Oh, he was sweet enough to her then, but I knew, yes I knew, as soon as he'd had her, it would be over for her. She'll come to no good, just like Tito's mother, who left a kid of not even two alone while she went whoring on Isla Maciel for that cabrón *whose name I can't remember. I used to take Tito into my bed to stop his crying the nights she was out. Then I gave him a bed in the corner of my room, so, when she didn't come back, he was used to me. I don't think he remembers her. He was too young.*

The dog lunged at the broom, trying to retrieve a piece of bread, and she almost tripped over it. "You watch out, Perro, or I'll tie you up again instead of having you under my feet." She'd tied the dog up for a week after it had almost bitten off El Dentista's hand, but it had strained at its rope and whined all day. Anything was better than that noise, and that stupid Dentista had probably deserved it anyway. "Maybe you should be tied up instead, Dentista. Next time, I hope the dog takes a bigger chunk out of you," she shouted in the direction of room 37 at the back – El Dentista's room.

No, it's not the way it used to be when Señor Rodríguez and the family lived here, before the yellow fever frightened people away from the river and we all moved from this house to the one in Barrio Norte. Yellow fever — the black vomit. Hundreds of people dead every day. They say that, at the worst of it, it was more than five hundred. Anyone who could afford to leave got out. Coffins were piled on corners, waiting for the funeral carriages to pick them up. Soon, the coffin makers couldn't keep up, so, even if you had the money to buy a coffin, you couldn't. Garbage carts collected corpses wrapped in drapes and buried them in pits. It's a wonder no one in this house died.

It's supposed to be my job to take care of Esteban, but how was I to know he'd end up mooning over that girl of El Puño's? My God! Never in my life did I imagine that would happen. Esteban would be better off dreaming of La Bonita. She's no beauty, but he can't see anyway, poor thing, so what does it matter what she looks like? La Bonita's the only one in this house besides me who has any sense. She showed up at the door one day and told me she needed a room. She wasn't dragged in off the streets like El Puño's girls, not her. She isn't half as good-looking as some of them, but she has the men running after her just the same. She was born just up the street on Defensa, but she's going farther in life than this barrio,* I can tell you. She says she's going to be a singer and an actress. I guess she learned a few things about fighting from the farm boys. She's tough, that one — the only one El Puño doesn't touch. I swear she would kill him if he tried. Even the dog leaves her alone.*

---

* neighbourhood

Eight months after they had all moved to the house in Barrio Norte to get away from the yellow fever, Señora Rodríguez came home early from shopping with her sister and found her husband and Gloria naked in the library. As if that weren't enough for La Señora to put up with, Gloria's belly soon started to grow. Gloria, Dolores, and La Renga were sent in shame back to the house in San Telmo. After Gloria's son – also named Esteban, after his father – was born, Señor Rodríguez came to visit them every Sunday for exactly three hours between one and four in the afternoon. He brought jewellery, new clothes, and sweets for Gloria and gave Dolores money to buy things for the boy.

One Sunday, El Señor didn't come. Instead, a short, fat man wearing a grey suit and a serious face arrived with money and a message that Señor Rodríguez would not visit them for the next two Sundays because his wife had died.

"You will see," said Gloria. "He is a man of honour. It was only because of her that he couldn't marry me. You will see. He will marry me now."

Three weeks later, on the third Sunday in October, Gloria prepared all morning for his visit. She put on every piece of jewellery he'd ever given her, the blue silk dress he'd brought for her birthday, and the white lace shawl he'd given her for Christmas, even though it was much too hot for a shawl that afternoon. She was ready to accept his proposal and assume the status to which she knew she was entitled.

That visit went exactly as all the previous visits had. Señor Rodríguez kissed his son and, as usual, gave Dolores an envelope containing money. He sat on the patio with Gloria and Esteban for half an hour, and they opened the presents he'd brought. Esteban pulled a wooden train set out of a big box. He was told to kiss his father and thank him. Gloria opened a small box that contained a silver necklace. Señor Rodríguez mentioned nothing about his wife's death or about marrying Gloria. Dolores brought them lunch, and after they'd eaten, Pepita took Esteban to her room and Dolores cleared up the lunch dishes. Gloria and Señor Rodríguez went upstairs to the library, where they spent the remaining time alone.

At exactly four o'clock, Gloria kissed Señor Rodríguez goodbye, closed the front door, and turned to face Dolores, who was unable to wait even one minute longer for the news of when her daughter was to become the next Señora Rodríguez.

"He can't marry me yet." Gloria said. "It's too soon. He's a man of honour. He is respecting the memory of his wife. Be patient. You will see. Only a little while longer now."

A year passed, and another year after that, and El Señor was still respecting his wife's memory. His visits became less and less frequent. Every Sunday, Gloria continued to prepare herself, even though it was often weeks between his appearances. Every Sunday, lunch was laid out on the table, the water was kept hot for the *mate*, and Gloria would sit in her blue dress and silver necklace, waiting for her future husband to arrive. She began to pace the corridor at night, unable to sleep, muttering to herself, "You will see. Only a few weeks now until he marries me. He is a man of honour."

And when it was no longer possible to deny that his son was steadily going blind – when the child was starting to stumble over his own feet and bump into things and could only see you when you were right in front of him – Señor Rodríguez stopped coming altogether. He sent his younger brother, Armando, to live in the house. Armando was a heavy-set bully with great black eyebrows that twitched when he was angry, which was often. He frightened everyone.

"It's hard to believe that this devil is El Señor's brother," Dolores would whisper over and over again to Pepita. "El Señor is a gentleman. The only jobs Armando has had in his life are drinking, chasing women, and betting on the horses. He's a good for nothing *baboso*.* How could El Señor have sent him here?" Then she would raise her eyes towards heaven, begging God to take this *malevo*† out of their lives and give them all some peace.

---

* fool
† bad guy

Armando would bellow orders from his room at the back of the first floor for Dolores or Pepita to bring him something to eat whenever he felt hungry. When he sat on the patio, drinking and smoking, Pepita would try not to look at him. His hands were huge and tobacco-stained, his fingernails filthy. His thick black hair resisted all his attempts to slick it back. No matter how much *gomina* he used, it fell in greasy strands over his forehead. His shirt was stretched so tight over his ever-expanding belly that it looked as if it would split at the seams.

Pepita could feel Armando watching her as she swept, washed dishes, and hung clothes to dry. After years of trying to ignore her body, she became self-conscious. She smoothed her skirt and made sure her blouse was tucked in. When she bent down to pick up the laundry basket, she would touch her top button to be sure it was fastened. Whenever Armando demanded she bring him food, she got Esteban to come with her. She hated being alone with Armando in that dark, smelly room of his, even for a minute. Late at night, she would hear him lurching, drunk, along the corridor, bumping into things and cursing. Sometimes his footsteps would slow down just outside her door, and she held her breath and her heart pounded until she heard him move on.

Armando had given the man they called El Dentista, named for his mouthful of crooked teeth, the room beside his. El Dentista ran errands for Armando – bought him cigarettes and placed his bets on the horses. Armando brought other men to the house, some more frightening than himself, with scars on their faces and knives tucked into their belts. They huddled in corners, drinking whiskey and grappa, or swaggered around the patio, starting fights. On Saturday nights, men came with guitars, a *bandoneón*, and their women with tight dresses, painted lips, and curses for everyone. Pepita would sit with Esteban in the corridor on the second floor overlooking the patio, watching through the railing, listening and describing the scene to him, unable to take her eyes off those women.

Gloria cut the bottoms off the skirts that El Señor had given her, so her legs showed. She started to wear lipstick. Dolores looked as if she would explode.

"Haven't you brought enough dishonour on this family without painting your face and hanging around with these *malevos* from the street? Don't you have any shame, Gloria? You have no husband and an illegitimate child who's going blind, poor thing, forcing us all to live in this house with these animals. My God! It would be better to have La Renga as a daughter than go through this."

"At least those men don't care if I have one kid or ten. At least we have this house. And I remind you, Mother dear, this dishonour that you keep complaining about is what gives you a roof over your head and food in your stomach. And don't think for a minute that the stupid cripple wouldn't let any one of those men who'd have her do whatever he wanted with her."

Gloria's dresses got tighter. She started smoking. Pepita thought Gloria looked magnificent. Her scarlet lips, her silky hair that was swept back into a knot at just the right place at the nape of her neck, those beautiful legs showing through the slit in the side of her dress as she danced with one man, then another, and yet another.

"Che, *cabrón*, what are you afraid of, son of a bitch?" Pepita would practice the curses in front of the long mirror that hung on the back of the door in her room. The mirror had a crack running down its centre. Silent curses, invisible makeup. In those moments, she was a beauty with two perfect, long, straight legs, desired by every man. Some nights, she dreamed her legs were as splendid as Gloria's, and when she woke up, she'd lie very still, holding onto the feeling of having those two beautiful legs. The moment she moved, the dream would be over.

One night, Armando's footsteps stopped outside Pepita's door, and that time, the door opened. In the dim light coming from the corridor, she could see the great black hulk of his body. The door closed, and in the darkness, she could hear his breath, smell it, taste it. An acrid mix of whiskey, stale tobacco, and vomit. She lay very still, praying he would go away. Before she could scream, he had one hand over her mouth, the other around her throat, and he was on top of her.

She fought for air, squeezed her eyes shut so tight they hurt, dug her fingernails into the mattress, into him, into herself. The pain between her legs seared up into her stomach. Armando's mouth was pressed right against her ear and all she could hear was the sound of his breathing. All she could feel was the pain. Again and again. She wished him dead, wished herself dead. But, just at the moment she was sure she would die if he didn't stop, in the middle of one of his terrible short, sharp grunts, he abruptly pulled himself away.

"Son of a bitch! What are you doing in here, you fucking kid?" Armando rolled off Pepita, landing with a thud on the floor. "What kind of *puta* life is this, when I can't even fuck a miserable girl anymore without the blind bastard kid of my shit of a brother getting in the way?"

Pepita forced her eyes open in time to see Armando stumbling out of the doorway, pulling his pants up with one hand. Standing beside the bed was Esteban, looking straight into her face as if he could see her, had seen everything. He sat down on the bed beside her.

"It's all right, Esteban. Go back to bed and please close the door."

After the boy had gone, she buried her face in her

pillow, and her whole body shook until her stomach hurt and her face was wet with enough tears to wash away Armando's sour saliva. And then she imagined Armando in the middle of his sweating and snorting, lifting his head and finding himself staring straight into Esteban's serious face, and she laughed so hard she thought she would stop breathing.

∞

"Dance with me, Renga." El Dentista grabbed the broom from La Renga and danced it around the patio.

"Go to the devil, Dentista. You're almost seventy and still driving me crazy!" In the fifty years since Armando had brought him to the house, El Dentista had lost most of his hair and looked thinner and wirier every day. The only thing that hadn't changed was that mouthful of teeth. He'd managed to keep every single one of them. He looked like an underfed rat.

"I clean up after you all day, you crazy old man! Don't expect me to dance with you too. And give me back that broom, unless you're going to use it for once in your useless life."

"Give me a kiss, Renga. Just one. Right here." El Dentista puckered his lips and blew kisses at her, holding the broom just out of her reach. The dog bared its teeth and growled.

"You can kiss my ass, *cabrón*. Kiss yourself if you

can stand it. Or perhaps you'd like to kiss the dog."

"Oh, come on, Renga, dance with me."

Years ago, Pepita had sometimes let herself imagine, just for a moment, that these were not just taunts, that one or another of them really wanted to dance with her. She'd stopped having those dreams a long time ago.

Gloria was gone. Many other girls with beautiful legs had come and gone, but she, La Renga, was still there. When she walked, her right leg swung outward, and when it landed, she moved forward with a little hop. After almost seventy years of practice, it was as smooth as a dance step, even if that leg did feel a little heavier every year and it was getting harder to ignore the pain in her hips. *Pata loca*, crazy foot, La Renga's dance. She'd heard the jokes so often that they meant nothing now.

EL CIEGO

Acaricia mi ensueño
El suave murmullo de tu suspirar.
Como ríe la vida
Si tus ojos negros me quieren mirar.[*]

"*He was the son of Señor Rodríguez, so Armando was his uncle.*
His mother, Gloria, was kind of crazy, so Doña Pepa took care
of him. I helped him too. He was blind. That's why everyone
called him El Ciego, but his real name was Esteban, like his
father."

∞

When he was a boy, the colours drained out of the
world around Esteban slowly, steadily, as if someone

---

[*] The soft murmur of your sigh / Caresses my dreams. / How life
would laugh / If your dark eyes wanted to look at me. (From the
tango "El Día Que Me Quieras." 1935. Music: Carlos Gardel.
Lyrics: Alfredo Le Pera.)

37

were turning down a lamp. He was left with only a child's memory of colour, shape, and dimension. He recognized people and their intentions by sounds and smells, and sometimes there were things he could not understand, things he found impossible to imagine.

Little Tito was his eyes. He brought Esteban cigarettes and led him from his room to the patio downstairs, where they sat drinking *mate* in the afternoons before the patio was filled with the sounds of the guitars and the *bandoneón* and the *malevos* with their knives and bottles of grappa, whiskey, and *ginebra*. Later, when the dancers arrived, Tito would describe them. "The bald guy always steps on the fat girl's foot, and the skinny guy with the white scarf is getting too drunk to dance. I think he might fall over."

Tito also told him about the people who lived in the other rooms. El Loco, the crazy guy in number 22, was teaching him to read. El Dentista, the skinny one with the bad teeth in number 37, gave him money to buy his lottery tickets. Armando in number 14 had come in drunk again late last night. La Niña Bonita was in number 15. "They say she's not pretty at all, but she is funny." Los Gallegos, the Spanish family in number 55. "They all have the same long face." And La Chica, El Puño's girl.

Sometimes La Chica passed them on the patio, and Esteban would hear the rustle of a shopping bag, her feet on the tile floor, her laugh. He counted her steps up the stairs to the second floor, smelled jasmine, and imagined her buying the flowers from Julieta at the corner.

"Describe her to me, Tito?"

"She's skinny. I guess she's pretty. I don't know, señor. She smells nice. She smiles at me. El Puño isn't very nice to her. Sometimes he pushes her or smacks her around."

El Puño had picked La Chica up somewhere on the street and brought her to La Renga, who had let her have the room beside Esteban's. Esteban could hear them at night. The sounds should have been gentle, the words should have caressed – *cortejar, galantear, hacer el amor*, to make love. Instead, he would hear one voice that was soft, light, pleading and another, heavy and threatening, winding tighter and tighter into a dangerous fistful of words. He didn't feel right about listening, but many nights, it was hard to ignore what was going on in the next room.

Sometimes he could hear her crying, so softly that, at first, he had thought she was humming. He didn't sleep those nights, wanted to tell her she wasn't alone, that he was just in the next room. One night, he dreamed he opened her door and lifted her lightly, easily out of there – for she weighed no more than a child – and brought her to his room. In the mornings after El Puño left, he would sometimes hear her singing or the clatter of a spoon against a plate, and he would smell *mate*.

One morning, he opened his door and the scent of spring poured in. Her door must have been open too because he could hear her singing as clearly as if they were in the same room. He hummed along. Tito had already brought him some hot water. He poured some into his *mate*[c] and sat on the edge of his bed. Life was just as it should be. His ears strained to catch every sound, every sigh, every movement, every note. He didn't want to miss anything.

∞

The dancers were gathering on the patio downstairs. Tito had gone to find cigarettes to sell to the men. Esteban could hear the first notes of the *bandoneón*. The guitar joined in. La Bonita yelled at someone to keep his hands to himself. More shouting. La Renga's dog barked.

"*Che*, don't keep that bottle all for yourself. Give me a drink."

"Where are the girls?"

"I'm first, brother."

"Go to the devil!"

"Give me that bottle!"

"Music, *maestro*!"

Esteban heard boots on the stairs. El Puño's boots.

---

[c] container used for drinking *mate*

He counted the steps. More notes were squeezed from the *bandoneón*. The boots reached the top of the steps and moved along the corridor to the door beside his.

"No! I'm not going down there. Don't touch me!" La Chica's voice.

The back of a hand on the side of a face.

"No! Please, no!"

Something cracked against the tiles, bounced off the stone sill in her doorway, rolled along the corridor. A *mate*.

"No! Leave me alone!"

In the corridor, the thud of flesh and bone against stone.

"*Cabrón*! Get out. Go to hell and never come back!"

"Shut up, whore! I'll come back whenever I feel like it."

The sound of El Puño's boots along the corridor and down the stairs were lost in the midst of the clapping, the shuffling of the dancers' feet, and the driving beat of the *bandoneón,* until it was no more than a part of the tango. Below on the patio, people clapped, the dancers' feet brushed the tiles, a baby howled.

Esteban waited, listened. He felt his way out to the corridor. He swept his feet from side to side, determined to find the *mate*. He went down on his hands and knees, searching the floor, and found it lodged against the railing. He stood up and felt his way back to the third column of the railing – the one with

41

the rough patch of rust as big as his hand that was right across from La Chica's room. Her door was open and the air from the room was heavy with sweat, *mate*, grappa, tobacco, fear. And jasmine.

"*Hola.*"

Silence.

"*Hola*? Señorita?"

"What?" Her voice was thin, fragile, like broken glass.

"I have your *mate.*"

"Who is it?"

"It's me, Esteban."

"Esteban?"

"El Ciego. I have your *mate*. I found it out here in the corridor. Would you like me to bring it in for you?"

"Oh…no, it's OK."

"I'll leave it here, then." He put the *mate* on the doorsill.

"Oh…OK, yes. Thank you, Esteban."

"You're welcome, señorita. Goodnight."

"Goodnight, Esteban."

He pulled the door shut. This had been their first conversation. She had spoken his name. He slept well that night.

Esteban woke to La Renga cursing the dog, those sons of a thousand whores who danced and drank all night on the patio, her miserable life. Tito brought him cigarettes and told him yes, the *mate* was still on the sill outside La Chica's door. Esteban hadn't heard her singing that morning. He sent Tito to find La Bonita.

La Bonita's shoes along the corridor. La Chica's door sliding open.

"*Che, piba!* Wake up, girl! What happened here? My God!" He heard La Bonita run back along the corridor, shouting for Doña Pepa to come, come now, and didn't she have any idea about what went on in this house, for the love of God?

Almost everyone was on the patio, all shouting at once about what to do. Tito and La Bonita watched from the corridor upstairs, outside El Ciego's room.

"Someone should call the police," La Renga said. "It was that worthless piece of shit, El Puño, who did it. He was up there last night."

"And just who is going to call the cops, Renga? Armando growled. "I hope you're ready to face that *malevo* and his friends when they find out you did?"

"Don't say anything, Renga, or we'll all be in trouble," said one of Los Palitos.

"She was asking for it anyway, hanging around with him," said the other one.

"Besides, she was still alive when El Puño left her room. I heard her. I swear it. She was shouting at him upstairs. '*Cabrón*, go to hell and don't ever come back!' That's what she said."

"Yeah, that's what she said. Then I saw him coming down the stairs."

"I heard her too, and I saw him coming down the stairs."

"Me too."

"Yeah! So he might not have done it."

"It could have been any of those sons of whores she hung around with."

"Yeah, any one of them!"

"But El Ciego was right next door. He must know what happened."

"El Ciego. What could a blind man see? No, they won't believe him."

"I don't want those *malevos* coming after me for passing on some story to the cops that I heard from a blind guy."

The dog barked and Armando threw a chair at it.

"All of you, just keep your mouths shut! If anyone goes to the cops, we're all dead!"

La Bonita went into El Ciego's room and sat on the chair beside his bed.

"Nobody will say anything, you know," she said. "As soon as El Puño and his men find out, they'll come and take her body away and probably dump it in the river, so no one will ever know anything."

"Yes. Do you know the girl's name?"

"No. Nobody does. I think she came from the provinces. Salta, maybe."

"What is your real name?"

"Laura."

"My name is Esteban."

Esteban heard her skirt rustle as she stood up. She put a *mate* into his hands. "Perhaps this is yours, Esteban. Tito found it in the corridor."

"No, it isn't. Mine is on the table beside my bed, where I always leave it."

"Well, maybe you could just keep this one here until we find out who it belongs to."

"Yes, OK." He cradled the *mate* gently in his hands.

Esteban knew he might be the only one who would remember La Chica and all the mornings they'd sung together, drunk *mate* together. She had spoken his name, but he would never know hers.

EL DENTISTA

Por una cabeza de un noble potrillo
Que justo en la raya afloja al llegar
Y que al regresar parece decir
No olvides, hermano,
Vos sabés no hay que jugar.
Por una cabeza, metejón de un día
De aquella coqueta y risueña mujer.[*]

"*They all told me stories, especially El Dentista. His real name was Héctor. He was skinny and, even when I was a kid, he looked short. Whenever he told me anything, he made me promise not to tell anyone else. He had a lot of secrets. He liked to bet on the horses and he taught me how to play the lottery. He used to*

---

[*] Losing by a head of a noble horse / That slacks off in the final stretch. / And when it comes back, it seems to say / Don't forget, brother, / You know you don't have to play. / Losing by a head, crazy love / Of that flirtatious, smiling woman. (From the tango "Por una Cabeza." 1935. Music: Carlos Gardel. Lyrics: Alfredo Le Pera.)

drive Doña Pepa crazy. But he was Armando's friend, so she couldn't kick him out."

∞

Héctor pedalled furiously away from the racetrack, his heart pounding so hard he felt it would leap out of his chest, as if by pedalling fast enough, he could fly out of the city of Buenos Aires into the provinces and hide until everyone had forgotten about him. The bicycle was too small for him, and when he pedalled, his knees came almost to his chest. When he reached Retiro Station, he would have taken the next train in any direction if he'd had any money. But he'd lost it all – everything El Chino had given him, right down to the last centavo. He'd put it all on one horse, which had lost by a head. This was supposed to have been the race that would make him rich and give him the courage to speak to the girl and make her notice him. But all that was lost now – the money, the girl, and maybe even his life if El Chino caught him.

This wasn't the first time Héctor had used the winnings from one race to bet on a later one, but by the end of the day, he'd always managed to make the money back, with usually at least a little left over for himself.

It was seeing the girl that made him risk it all that day. He'd seen her at the races many times before, always with another girl and two men – one who looked about the same age as the girls and one much older. She was so beautiful – a slim, fragile flower. Was the smile on her lips, that look as he passed her, meant for him? Surely it must have been because wasn't she looking right at him? After watching her for months, he finally learned her name when he was standing in the line at the betting windows that day. He turned his head and there she was, just a few short steps away from him. He could feel his heart pounding in his chest.

"Uncle, I want to bet on number six in the second race." She laughed as if she'd never had a worry in the world.

"Number six!" The other girl snorted. "That bag of bones? You must be crazy, Claudia! I'm betting on Resbaloso. Everyone knows he's going to win."

"Yes, of course it's going to be Resbaloso. Don't you think so, Uncle?" the young man said. The older man smiled and gave him some money, and the young man joined the line behind Héctor.

When Héctor's turn came at the window, instead of putting El Chino's money on Resbaloso to win or place in the second race as he was supposed to, he put it on number six to win and Resbaloso to place.

In the second race, six was the winner by a head, followed by Resbaloso. After calculating what he owed El Chino, Héctor still had plenty of money for himself.

The girl – Claudia – had brought him luck.

Once, he'd followed the four of them from the racetrack, walking his bicycle a block behind them, and saw them go into a café on Juncal. He stood across the street, smoking his last cigarette as slowly as possible, making conversation with the man in the newspaper kiosk while watching them through the window of the café. He left his bicycle beside the kiosk and crossed the street, stealing glances at them as he passed the café window. He went halfway around the block and then turned and walked back. He crossed the street and pretended to look at the hats in a shop window, which had a mirror in which he could watch their reflection. After Claudia and the other girl finished their pastries and the men put out their cigarettes, Héctor crossed the street again and strolled past the café window for one last look. He waited at the corner for them to pass and followed them along Juncal and onto Sinclair to a house with a small rose garden in front. The breeze carried the scent of the flowers, and he could hear Claudia laughing as the front door closed. For the rest of his life, he would never smell roses without imagining her laughter.

After that, on his way to the racetrack, he would always ride to Sinclair, where he would get off his bicycle and walk past Claudia's house, hoping for a glimpse of her, imagining he was stepping exactly where she had walked.

Héctor felt the money bulging in his pocket. He walked back to the betting window, emptied his pockets, and bet everything on the long shot in the third race. He needed to win big – enough to pay for seats in the *tribuna oficial*. That would show all those snobs with their hair slick with *gomina* and their polished leather shoes. He would buy a new jacket and tie and take Claudia to sit right up there at the finish line with him.

Héctor wished his parents were still alive to see it all. He would have bought his father a new suit, and his mother would be wearing a new dress, gloves, and hat. He imagined them sitting beside him and Claudia in one of the box seats that were reserved for families. After the race, they would all go to the café and have tea and cake served on a silver tray.

When Héctor was a baby, his father, Emilio, had brought them to Buenos Aires from Uruguay with dreams of a better life. He found a job in a tannery on the banks of the Riachuelo and a home for his family in a *conventillo* in Dock Sur with fifteen other families. He would arrive home smelling of rotten meat and other acrid smells that Héctor didn't recognize. The skin on his father's hands was red and cracked, and at night, Héctor could hear him coughing. Eleven years later, Emilio's dream died with him when he collapsed on the floor of the tannery. One morning a few months after that, Héctor's mother didn't wake up. At thirteen,

Héctor found himself on the street with not a soul in the world who cared whether he lived or died.

Héctor watched the third race from the cheapest seats in the grandstand, which didn't have a good view of the finish line. The horses were neck and neck as they approached it and, at first, it was hard to be sure which horse had won. But very soon, he knew he was finished. El Chino would find out that his horse had come first in the opening race, but he wouldn't know that his winnings had gone on the long shot in the third race. El Chino had eyes and knives in every corner of Buenos Aires. Héctor knew, no matter how fast or in which direction he rode, there was nowhere to hide.

Armando Rodríguez was his only hope. By some stroke of luck, Héctor hadn't managed to collect money from him for the horses that week. If Armando gave him money for the next race day, there might be a chance of winning back what he owed El Chino, and if he could dodge El Chino for a few days, he might just come out of this alive.

Time was what he needed. He headed for San Telmo. Armando could usually be found in the bar in the Plaza del Comercio.*

Through the window of the bar, Héctor could see Armando's broad back and his mass of greasy black

---

* Renamed the Plaza Dorrego in 1905.

hair. He was at his usual table, already drunk, a cigarette stuck to his lower lip, leaning forward unsteadily, waving his huge hands around and shouting at the man behind the bar. He'd never had to work, thanks to his older brother's money. He spent his time smoking, drinking, and getting fat, but at least he wasn't too dangerous. He backed down from a fight with anyone who might have a chance of winning. Héctor propped his bicycle against a lamppost and went into the bar.

"*Hola*, Armando."

"*Che*, Dentista. What's up?" No matter how many times he'd heard this nickname, Héctor still hated it. He passed his hand over his mouth, self-conscious, and ran his tongue over his crooked teeth. In spite of the fact that his mouth had room for fewer teeth than normal, he had two extra eye teeth, which had forced the others to grow in unusual directions.

"Sit down, Dentista. Have a drink and tell me why you didn't come to pick up money from me for the *burros,* you son of a bitch. I bet that *cabrón,* El Chino, made a pile of cash this week." Armando slapped him on the shoulder, signalled to the waiter to bring another glass, and stuck a cigarette into Héctor's mouth.

"That's why I came to see you now, so you don't miss your chance next time. Resbaloso placed today, just as you said."

"Did I say that? Good! Now I'm feeling lucky. I'm

going to put down more money this week, maybe double." Armando lit Héctor's cigarette. Héctor sucked in the smoke, did some quick mental calculations, and felt his panic receding. As soon as they finished their drinks, Armando ordered more.

At three in the morning, Armando was slumped over the table and the bartender was washing the last of the glasses. "I'm ready to close. I'll help you get him outside. I've taken him home more times than I can count. You can do it tonight."

Together, they got Armando to his feet, dragged him outside, and leaned him against the lamppost beside Héctor's bicycle. Héctor locked his knees and wedged his shoulder under Armando's armpit, pushing upwards as hard as he could to prevent Armando from sliding to the ground.

"He lives on Defensa, just before San Juan. You can see the house from here." The bartender pointed to a large house down the street. "If he can't manage to unlock the door himself, you'll probably find keys in his back pocket. Or knock and La Renga will show you where to deposit him." He went back into the bar and locked the door.

"Come on, Armando. I'll take you home. Walk with me." It was becoming increasingly difficult to keep Armando's sagging body upright.

"Walk! I can hardly even stand up."

"No problem. I'll help you. Lean on the bicycle."

Héctor wrestled Armando towards the front of the bicycle and propped his massive chest on the handlebars. When he moved the bicycle, Armando lurched sideways, almost taking them both down.

"*Che*, Dentista, son of a bitch, watch what you're doing!"

"It's OK, Armando, just keep walking. The bicycle will hold you up." Héctor pushed with all his strength against Armando's bulk and moved the bicycle forward. They progressed unsteadily along Defensa, Héctor struggling to maintain their precarious balance. They veered left, right, and left again, narrowly missing two lampposts and a dog.

"That wheel going round is making me dizzy, Dentista."

"Don't look at it. Keep your eyes on the houses. Look up at the sky. Don't worry. I'll steer. I'm used to bicycles." If they kept moving, they might make it.

"You're a good man, Dentista. I think you're going to bring me luck. I'm going to bet triple on the *burros* next time." This gave Héctor the strength to negotiate the last few steps to Armando's house.

Armando fumbled in his pockets and turned them inside out. "Shit, I've lost the keys!" He fell against the door and hammered on it with his fist. "Somebody come and let me in!" But there was only silence from inside the house. He became more and more furious and kicked at the door. "Renga, come and open this *puta* door!"

After several minutes of Armando's pounding on the door, Héctor heard a woman's voice. "Yes, who's there?"

"You know damn well who it is, Renga. Stop playing games and open this fucking door or I'll kick it down and knock your head off."

The heavy door creaked open a crack. A thin young woman with a tattered shawl wrapped around her shoulders eyed them suspiciously.

Armando shoved the door open, almost knocking the woman over. When she wouldn't move, Armando managed to summon enough coordination to push her aside and drag Héctor and the bicycle through the door.

"This is my friend El Dentista, the only good man in all of Buenos Aires. He's coming in to have some *mate* with me and I don't want to hear anything from you about it, Renga. I'm the one who makes the rules in this house." Armando staggered backwards and threw his arm around Héctor's shoulders. They would both have collapsed if Héctor hadn't braced himself. The bicycle clattered to the ground. In one of the rooms, a child started to cry.

"His room is that way." La Renga pointed to the back of the patio.

After hoisting Armando onto his bed, Héctor lay on

the long wooden bench on the opposite side of the room and rolled up his jacket to use as a pillow. His head was spinning with drink, adrenaline, and relief. That woman, La Renga, would keep the world out. He'd found a place to hide.

Héctor was woken up the next morning by the sound of his bicycle bell and some kids yelling. Armando's bed was empty.

He got up and opened the door and could see a boy of about twelve pushing the bicycle around the patio. Perched on the handlebars was a younger boy, who was ringing the bell. They were weaving shakily all over the place and almost collided with La Renga as she hobbled out of her room. Two skinny boys watched from the second floor.

"Juan, take Esteban off that bicycle!" La Renga shook her broom at them. "I'm sure his mother would like him to stay in one piece"

"His mother's crazy. She doesn't–"

"That's enough, Juan. Besides, Armando isn't going to be very happy if you break his friend's bicycle."

Héctor walked out onto the patio. "Good morning, señora." When Juan saw Héctor, he lost his grip on the handlebars and the bike and the boys came crashing down.

"Esteban! My God!" La Renga limped over to the younger boy. Juan dusted himself off and smirked.

"I'm OK, Doña Pepa. Please, I'm all right." Esteban tried to wriggle free of her, but she held on tight. After checking him for damage and finding nothing, she glared at Héctor.

"Señor—"

"It's all right, señora. I think these boys just need a few bicycle lessons." Héctor stood the bicycle up. "Who wants to go first?"

"No!" La Renga shook her head.

"Why not? Every boy should learn how to ride a bicycle."

"I'll go first," Juan said. "I tried it once. I can almost ride."

"OK, you pedal slowly and steer, and I'll help you keep your balance when you start. The important thing is to keep moving and not look down."

Juan hoisted himself onto the bicycle. Héctor held onto the back of the seat and, when the boy seemed to have his balance, gave the bicycle a gentle push and let go. Juan managed to continue pedalling almost the length of the patio before keeling over. After a few more tries, he was able to negotiate turns.

"Well done, Juan. Now it's Esteban's turn."

Silence. Juan scuffed his foot against the floor. Esteban stared straight ahead.

"No!" La Renga shook her head.

"Please, señor, let me try again." Juan said.

"Sure. After Esteban has a turn." Héctor patted the

bicycle seat. "Come on, kid."

"He can't ride a bike." Juan stared at his feet.

"I know he can't ride a bike. That's why I have to teach him. Neither could you an hour ago."

"Yes, but he really can't."

"Why not?"

"Because he'll bump into things. Because he… can't see."

Esteban scrambled to his feet. La Renga grabbed his arm and pulled him towards the stairs.

Héctor called after them, "Even people who can see sometimes bump into things."

"Please, señor. No!" La Renga clung onto Esteban.

"I promise he'll be OK, señora."

"Yes, I want to try," Esteban said.

"Esteban, no!"

"I want to try, Doña Pepa." Esteban pulled away from her and walked slowly towards Héctor, who helped him onto the bicycle seat. The boy's feet just reached the pedals.

"OK, kid. Remember that the important thing is to keep moving. If you do that, you won't lose your balance. Keep the handlebars straight. Control the bike. Don't let it control you."

They did a few turns around the patio, Héctor holding onto the back of the seat, giving instructions and guiding the bicycle as Esteban pedalled. When Héctor let go, Esteban sailed away, listed sideways, and crashed straight into the wall. La Renga shrieked.

Héctor ran over and helped Esteban up. "Get back on the bike. You have to do it right away before the fear has time to get you. Ready?"

Esteban nodded solemnly and Héctor helped him to get back on the bicycle.

"Don't worry. Start slowly. I'll tell you when to turn. OK, that's good, good." Héctor let go of the bicycle again, calling out directions. "Keep moving. Now go left. You don't want to run into the wall. Good, good. Now left again. Stay in a straight line now so you don't hit the table."

By the time Armando stumbled back into the house that afternoon, Esteban was able to ride almost all the way around the patio without falling.

It took El Chino's men less than twenty-four hours to find Héctor. That evening, when he went to meet Armando in the bar in the plaza, before he even knew anyone was behind him, he was slammed, face first, against the outside wall of the bar, one man on either side of him, both of his arms pinned halfway up his spine, gasping for air.

"Where is El Chino's money?"

"I…I don't have it on me. I got side-tracked. I was planning to go and look for him tomorrow." Héctor could feel the man's breath on the side of his face and tasted blood and dirt.

"This is a message from El Chino."

Héctor felt the cold metal of the knife slice into his belly, felt his legs give way, and heard the scuffling of feet. By the time he'd mustered enough breath to raise his head, the men were gone.

When Héctor first opened his eyes, he wasn't sure where he was. It was dark, and the air was heavy with the smell of grappa and tobacco smoke. He was sweating and his head ached. When he tried to sit up, pain seared through the right side of his body and he fell back. He drifted in and out of sleep, not knowing where his dreams began or ended. He heard a bicycle bell, a woman's voice. "He is an honourable man, he will marry me soon." Someone snoring, kids yelling, a man coughing. His father was beside the bed, pulling the blanket up over Héctor's chest. His father's hands were smooth, like worn leather. And sometimes Claudia was there, pressing a cool cloth that smelled of roses against his face.

"*Che*, Dentista. I see you've finally returned from the dead, brother." Armando was standing beside the bed. The light coming through the open door that led to the patio made Héctor squint.

"Armando." When he pushed himself up, the pain stabbed into his guts. "Shit!"

"Yeah, I bet you're feeling a little sore. Somebody

decided to go to work on you. Your pockets were empty. I guess he took what he could find." Armando shook his head slowly and snorted. "Lucky for you, he wasn't very good at the job, and lucky I found you before you died in the street like a rat. Here, have some grappa." He put the bottle to Héctor's lips.

Héctor's jaw hurt so much he could hardly open his mouth. He managed to swallow a mouthful before he flopped back.

"The doctor didn't think you would make it, but I guess you're tougher than you look. You've been out cold most of time for the last couple of days. Maybe now you're awake, I can have my bed back."

"I dreamed someone was washing my face. A woman."

"Hah! That was no dream. It was La Renga. Juan and that blind kid of Gloria's made sure she took good care of you. I've had a hard time keeping them out of here." Armando turned around and shouted into the patio. "Renga!"

No answer.

"Renga!"

"What?" A woman shouted back.

"El Dentista is with us again. Bring us something to eat. And don't forget more hot water for the *mate*."

Armando lit two cigarettes and stuck one into Héctor's mouth. A few minutes later, La Renga shuffled in with a kettle of hot water and put it on the table beside Armando's bed without looking at them. Behind her came Juan, carefully carrying two cups of soup, and Esteban with two spoons. Juan put the soup on the table and then took the spoons from Esteban, putting one in each cup. His eyes kept shifting to look at Héctor.

"We've been riding the bicycle, señor," Esteban said. "I hope that's OK."

"No problem. How's it going?"

"I can almost go around the patio by myself without falling."

"And I never fall," Juan said.

"That's good, then. I'll be up soon and you can show me."

"OK, boys, let's go." La Renga put her hand on Esteban's shoulder and turned him towards the door. She ushered the boys out to the patio.

Héctor pushed himself up onto his elbows, fighting the pain. "Thank you, señora. I'm sorry to have caused so much trouble."

La Renga stopped for a moment and called back over her shoulder. "It's no trouble, señor."

Armando walked to the door, cleared his throat, and spat onto the patio. "Hah! That witch is a lot better behaved with you around. I can hardly get her to do anything for me. And, whenever she does, she can't do it without a scowl on that miserable face of hers. Maybe you should move in, Dentista." He laughed. "Actually, that's not a bad idea. I like your company, and if you were here, I wouldn't miss any more chances on the *burros*. How about it? It looks as though you'll have to stay for a few more days anyway."

"Actually, I am looking for a new place to live."

"Good. Then it's settled. You can have the room next to mine. No one's using it."

"*Che*, Armando."

Armando lifted his head up from the table in the bar and tried to focus on the face of the man sitting across from him. He looked familiar, but all those *malevos* looked the same. A dark man in a suit, his hat pulled down low over his eyes, smoking a cigarette, a white scarf around his neck.

"Yeah, that's my name. Armando. Do I know you?"

"No."

"How do *you* know *me*?"

"Everyone knows you here." When the man smiled, he didn't look quite as dangerous.

Armando slapped the table and laughed. "Well, let me buy you a drink, brother. It's no fun drinking alone. Whiskey?"

The man nodded. "Thanks."

Armando signalled to the bartender, who brought another glass.

"So where's your friend tonight? The skinny little guy with the bicycle." The man took a packet of cigarettes out of his pocket and offered one to Armando.

"Aah, good cigarette. I like these." Armando lit both their cigarettes. "You must be talking about El Dentista."

The man nodded again.

Armando laughed. "The *pelotudo* got himself roughed up a few nights ago."

"What happened?"

"Somebody decided to feed him a mouthful of dirt and stick a knife in him. They didn't get much out of him, probably no more than a few pesos. He never has much money in his pockets unless it's after a race and he got lucky on the horses. Everyone around here knows that."

"So how is he?"

"I didn't think he'd make it, but the doctor patched him up, and it looks as if he'll live. He's a tough little son of a bitch." Armando laughed and drained his glass.

"Where is he now?"

"He's in my house, being waited on hand and foot, the little bugger!" Armando punched the edge of the table. "*Che, hermano*, if we're going to drink together, I'm going to have to call you something."

The other man exhaled smoke and took a long, slow sip of his drink. "They usually call me El Chino."

Armando swallowed hard and stared at the ashtray

as he slowly stubbed out his cigarette. "What are you doing in San Telmo?"

"Some business. With a mutual friend."

Armando cupped his chin in one hand, propping his head up. "A mutual friend?"

"Yeah, he owes me some money from Sunday's race." El Chino leaned over the table towards Armando, his arms crossed. The smoke from his cigarette curled up into Armando's face.

"Who is this mutual friend?"

"Your house guest."

"El Dentista?"

"Yes. And since you seem to have taken responsibility for him, I assume you're also responsible for his debts."

"What do you mean?" Armando drained his glass, silently cursing his own stupidity.

"I think you know exactly what I mean." El Chino ground out his cigarette beside Armando's elbow on the table, finished his drink, and stood up. He adjusted his white scarf. "Be in the Café El Estaño in La Boca tomorrow at eight o'clock with three hundred pesos. If you're not there, my friends and I will pay a visit to your house. Goodnight, Armando, and thanks for the drink. Say hello to your friend El Dentista for me."

Armando stormed across the patio and threw open the door to Héctor's room, ripping him out of a deep sleep.

"Wake up, Dentista, you son of a thousand whores!"

"What's the matter, Armando? What's—"

Armando grabbed Héctor by the front of his shirt and sat him up.

"Ow! Watch it! That hurts!"

"I should have let you die in the street, you little piece of shit!"

"What?"

"Shut up! I had a visit tonight from a friend of yours."

"A friend?"

"I told you to shut up."

'OK, Armando, just take it easy!"

"I had a visit from El Chino. He says you owe him money, and now he wants to get it out of me."

"Armando—"

"If I don't pay up, we're both dead. Next time, I think he'll finish the job properly. Shit! Now I'm going to have to go to my son-of-a-bitch brother for more money!"

"Armando, I'll pay you back. I promise!"

Armando's face was so close that Héctor couldn't bring it into focus. He had the front of Héctor's shirt clenched in his fist. When he let go, Héctor fell back onto the bed with a moan of pain.

"You bet you will, you miserable little turd!"

Héctor lay motionless, afraid to breathe.

Suddenly, Armando's mouth split into a smile and he began to laugh. He sat down on the bed and shook his head.

"One thing I have to say, Dentista, you cheating little son of a bitch, you've got guts. Not many people would have the nerve to play around with El Chino's money."

Armando spent the next day waiting. He waited the entire morning for his brother in the house in Barrio Norte. The housekeeper let him in and asked him to wait on the patio until Esteban was ready. It wasn't the first time he'd waited for his brother to make his entrance and ask, "How much this time, Armando?"

Armando always asked for a little more than he needed, to compensate for the humiliation. Esteban would wait only the time required for an answer before disappearing into the library and returning a few minutes later with the money, after which his carriage would take Armando back to San Telmo.

That night, Armando waited for El Chino in El Estaño. His fingers played nervously over the packet of money and the watch in his pocket. He checked the watch every few minutes and drank slowly, knowing he needed to have a clear head. Any mistake might be his last. By eleven o'clock, he'd finished all his cigarettes and El Chino still hadn't arrived. He ordered another drink and bought more cigarettes.

Just before midnight, two men came into the café and sat at the next table.

"*Che*, Roberto. Bring us some whiskey. We've got something to celebrate tonight."

The bartender brought their drinks. "What's up? What are you celebrating?"

"Somebody finally got that son of a thousand whores, El Chino. They were waiting for him on Isla Maciel this afternoon. They came up right behind him and stuck a knife in his kidneys."

Armando sucked so hard on his cigarette that he started to cough. He finished off his drink.

The bartender let out a slow whistle. "Who managed to do that?"

"There were two of them – one tall, skinny *malevo* and a little one. They say the little guy actually stuck the knife in."

"Is El Chino dead?" Armando lit another cigarette.

"Don't worry. They made sure of that. Nobody did anything until it was too late for that *cabrón*. They just watched him die. By then, the two guys were long gone. Nobody recognized them or, if anyone did, they're not saying."

"He's really dead, then?" Armando's hands were shaking.

"Yeah, brother, that's what I said. I tell you he's really dead."

After several more drinks, Armando staggered

home and fell into bed. A few minutes later, he heard his door creak open.

"*Che*, Armando. I was worried about you. Everything OK?"

"Yeah, yeah, everything's OK. Go back to bed, Dentista. I'm in no mood to have a conversation with you."

"Thanks, Armando. You know I'll pay you back."

"OK, OK, we'll talk about that later. Now move your bony ass out of here."

A couple of weeks later, Héctor decided it was time to go back to work. The sooner he started to pay Armando back, the better. Armando had given him some money for the horses, and now that El Chino was paid off, as long as he kept his eyes open, it was safe to go back to the racetrack.

Riding his bicycle was slightly easier than walking. By the time he reached Balvanera, the pain in his side had subsided into a dull ache and he'd forgotten about the money he owed and the trouble he was in. All he could think about was Claudia's face, her magical laugh, the roses in her garden.

First, he rode to the café on Juncal and looked through the window, but she wasn't there. Then he rode along Sinclair towards her house. And there she was, standing in the front garden. Alone. This was his chance to speak to her. He got off his bicycle and walked it towards her, whispering her name to himself over and over again.

Closer. He could see a watering can in her hand, the lace cuffs on her soft-green dress, the flash of a silver bracelet. *Claudia.* The tilt of her head, the curve of her chin. *Claudia.* Héctor took off his cap and smoothed his hair, holding his bicycle up with the other hand.

"Good afternoon, señorita."

She turned to look at him. Her smile quickly turned into a puzzled look. "Señor?" Her voice. All he wanted at that moment was to hear her voice again.

"My name is Héctor. You probably don't recognize me. I've seen you at the races." He twisted his cap and found it hard to concentrate on the words,

She shook her head. "No, I'm sorry. I don't remember you."

"No, I'm…I'm sure you don't. We've never spoken." Suddenly, he felt ashamed. When Claudia looked at him, it was as if she were shining a very bright light directly on him, lighting up every flaw – every crooked tooth, his bony arms, thin hair, shabby clothes, dirty cap, hands that were starting to look like his father's. He knew he'd never had a handsome face. He was almost twenty and had only kissed a girl once, when he was seventeen, in the alley behind her parents' bakery. Her name was Pamela. She was fat and smelled of flour. She said he had bad breath and refused to let him kiss her again, which he didn't mind because he hadn't enjoyed kissing her anyway and was relieved he wouldn't have to do it again.

He wished he could stop thinking of Pamela at that moment. He pushed a strand of hair out of his eyes and struggled to think of something, anything, to say to Claudia.

"Well…I…" He pushed the bicycle a little closer.

She took a step backwards. "I have to go inside now."

"Yes, yes, of course. Yes. I–"

"Goodbye."

"Goodbye, señorita." He put his cap back on and swung his leg over the bicycle seat, ignoring the pain that shot down his right side. He knew that his dream of her sitting beside him in the *tribuna oficial* was over. But he also knew he would risk it all again if he could, if only for that one terrible moment when she'd actually spoken to him.

Armando's horse came first in the second race. Héctor went to the window to collect the winnings. He put all the money into his pocket except for three pesos, which he put on the favourite for the next race. He was back in business. And, as they said, no matter where you sit, the bets are still the same.

"He is an honourable man. He is just respecting her memory." The swish of a skirt, the click of heels along the upstairs corridor. Héctor had heard the woman his first night here, and her voice had seeped into his fevered dreams the night El Chino's men had almost killed him.

"That's Señora Gloria, Esteban's mother." Juan whispered to Héctor. "She's completely crazy."

La Renga turned away and concentrated on sweeping dirt from the corner of the patio.

"You will see. He will marry me soon. That is why I have this house and all of you have a place to live." Gloria descended the stairs slowly, regally, and walked across the patio. La Renga poked her broom harder into the corner.

"She still thinks Señor Armando's brother is coming to marry her, but everyone knows he's not. My father says she's been waiting for ten years." Juan sniffed.

"He is an honourable man. Esteban? Esteban, where are you?" Gloria stretched out her hand.

"Señor Armando's brother's name is Esteban too." Juan said.

They could see the boy through the railing on the second floor. He felt his way down the stairs and across the patio, guided by the sound of his mother's voice.

"Esteban, I am waiting."

Gloria's son stood in front of her, expectant, but she looked right through him as if he weren't there. Then she straightened her skirt, patted her hair, and walked away, muttering to herself. Her pale, delicate hand gripped the railing as she went back up the stairs, and Héctor thought of his mother's hands, red and swollen from washing other people's clothes.

"I guess she forgot she named her son Esteban too." Juan giggled. "She always does that. I don't know why he doesn't just ignore her."

"Because she's his mother," Héctor said. "*Che*, Esteban, how about a ride on the bicycle?"

For once, La Renga had nothing to say.

It was the delight on Esteban's face that made Héctor decide he wouldn't tell Armando yet that he'd found out El Chino had been killed on Isla Maciel a few hours before Armando went to meet him in La Boca. News like that spread fast. Besides, he had no idea where else to go. As long as Armando didn't know he knew, El Dentista was safe for a while.

LA NIÑA BONITA

"Her real name was Laura, but they called her La Niña Bonita, the pretty girl. I think it was a joke because they didn't think she was very pretty. But she was nice to me and I liked talking to her. She was a good singer too, and she liked to sing my songs. I was the one who opened the door when she came to the house the first time. I'm happy I did."

∞

After three years of living with cows, no matter how many times she washed and scrubbed her body and her clothes, Laura could still smell them. She hadn't minded it so much when she was surrounded by them on Señor González' *estancia,** but only when she was on the crowded train back to Buenos Aires. After three years of breathing shit, cleaning up shit, eating shit, and taking shit, she had been dumped at the train station in

---

* ranch

Magdalena with some stale bread, a jar of water, a few pesos, and a tattered map of Buenos Aires that Celia, Señor González' cook, had given her.

When Laura was five, her mother had taken her to live in an orphanage. She could remember insisting to the nuns that she had a mother and there had been a mistake. It took her a long time to realize that there had been no mistake. Four years later, after a fever and nights of coughing until she thought her chest would burst, the nuns told her she would be going to the country. Sister Francisca would take her on the train to Magdalena, where a man and a boy with a horse and cart would be waiting to take her to the *estancia*.

When she arrived at the house in Magdalena, she was taken down a dark corridor to a small room at the back by the housekeeper, Constanza, a tall, thin woman with a long, serious face. Laura was surprised to find Luisa, one of the girls who had also lived in the orphanage, sitting on one of the two single beds. Luisa had disappeared one day, and none of the girls knew what had happened to her.

Laura remembered how Luisa would hide under her bed in the dormitory at the orphanage, crying for her mother. One of the nuns, usually Sister Francisca, would drag her out to the laundry room, still sobbing. One morning, as Luisa was standing on a chair and stirring the clothes around with the long wooden paddle, she leaned too far over the big tub of rinse water and fell in. After being hauled out by two of the older girls, she stood in the centre of the room, soaked and shivering. Sister Francisca wrapped a sheet around her and carried her out. Luisa's bed was empty for a couple of days until a new girl arrived.

Before she arrived at the *estancia*, Laura had never seen a cow in her life. At first, they frightened her with their great heads that swung around when she didn't expect it, their tails like ropes that whipped her when she milked them, and their hooves that left bruises on her arms and legs if she didn't move out of their way fast enough.

She was beaten by Humberto and the other stable boys if she spilled even a single drop of milk when she carried the heavy buckets or if she left too many twigs in the *mate* leaves after the harvest. Some nights, her whole body hurt and it was hard to fall asleep.

Humberto and the boys talked a lot about Buenos Aires and how they would live there one day. Humberto's father, who was in charge of the stables, went to the city once in a while. No one knew what exactly he did there, but there was talk of girls and music, and he usually came back with a few tangos and some money in his pockets. He liked to sing while he was working, even if he didn't have a very good voice.

Some nights, Laura could hear the music from the

gramophone in the González' house. She and Luisa would sneak behind the boys to the windows so they could hear the words. Laura memorized the lyrics and let the tangos run through her before she went to sleep. They helped take her mind off the pain.

When she said, "I'm from Buenos Aires and I'm going back there," the boys laughed.

"And just what are you going to do there?"

"Yeah, what?"

"I will sing the tango."

Enrique González snorted. "Girls don't sing the tango, especially fat, ugly ones like you." He laughed so hard that he looked as though he would split.

"Shut up, Enrique!" Laura swung her fist at him, but he jumped out of the way before the punch landed.

"You shut up, or I'll tell my father and you'll be in trouble. You should be grateful for what you have here. You have nowhere else to go. You're lucky he's so generous."

Enrique González never missed a chance to boast. "My father has invited Señor Villoldo to our house," he announced. "He writes and sings tangos. He's very famous and an important friend of my father's."

The night Villoldo arrived, while Laura was in the kitchen helping Celia prepare the evening meal, there was a sudden rainstorm. One of the carts carrying a load of *mate* leaves had gotten stuck in a muddy ditch.

Two of the boys were pushing the cart and another two were pulling the horse. Humberto was sitting in the cart and lashing the horse with a whip. It refused to budge. They were shouting and swearing so loud that Señor González, Enrique, and Villoldo came out of the house and ran down the hill to see what was happening. They were followed by Constanza, who was trying to hold an umbrella over Señor González' head so he wouldn't get wet, and Celia, who was still holding a carrot she'd been peeling. Laura ran behind Celia.

"That horse needs some encouragement, boys, not shouting and beating!" Villoldo turned to Celia. "Kindly give me that carrot, señora. And you, boy, get down from the cart and give me that whip you've been beating the poor horse with." He took the whip from Humberto and wrapped the leather line around the carrot. Then he climbed up into the seat and dangled the carrot just in front of the horse's nose. Its nostrils twitched. Villoldo extended his arm so the carrot was a little further away. The horse stretched its neck towards it and moved forward. The cart shuddered and the wheels turned slightly.

"Push, boys! Behind the cart. Now! Help the horse. Come on, you too, kid. Don't just stand there!" Villoldo shouted at Enrique, who slipped and fell as he ran towards the back of the cart. When he pushed himself up, he had mud all over his best suit. Laura put her hand over her mouth to stop laughing. Celia winked, which made Laura want to laugh even harder.

"Señor *Caballo,* don't you want that juicy carrot? Just move forward a bit and it's yours." Villoldo coaxed the horse, which stretched, strained, shook its head, and whinnied. The boys dug their feet into the mud and pushed. After about ten minutes, with a desperate lurch forward, the horse finally managed to pull the cart out of the ditch. Villoldo got down from the seat. He stroked the horse's nose and fed it the carrot. The boys cheered.

"What? Do you boys think I'm only good for singing tangos? I do this kind of work in Buenos Aires all the time. It's one of my other jobs." Villoldo looked straight at Humberto. "All a creature needs is a little encouragement and a push sometimes. When a horse sees a carrot, he has a reason to try harder. If not, he stays stuck in the mud. Beating never helps. You won't need this now." He threw the whip back to Humberto.

Señor González slapped Villoldo on the back and they walked back towards the house, followed by a bedraggled Enrique, who was sliding on the muddy ground, trying to keep up with his father.

"His Highness will certainly need a bath tonight," Celia whispered to Laura.

After dinner, while Celia and Laura were cleaning up the kitchen, they could hear Villoldo singing, accompanying himself on the guitar. Celia wiped her hands on her apron, put her finger to her lips, and motioned to Laura to be very quiet. She silently opened the kitchen door a crack, just wide enough for Laura to see, with one eye, Villoldo entertaining the González family and their friends with "El Choclo," a tango that would become more important for her than she knew at that moment.

"He only gets away with singing those words because everyone thinks it's only about a corn cob, but it's really about something else." Celia muttered.

"What's he really singing about, Celia?"

"Never mind, Laurita. You're too young to know about that yet. Come on. We've got a lot of work to do before we can sleep tonight."

One day, after three years of beatings, Laura knew she couldn't take one more. That was also the day Enrique, that *boludo*[*] son of Señor González, tried to stick his miserable hand up her skirt just because that idiot Luisa had let him do it, and Laura slammed her fist so hard into his belly she thought it would go right through him. He ran crying to his father. Señor González decided she was more trouble than she was worth and he would send her back to the nuns in Buenos Aires.

"Sister Francisca will be at the station. Wait on the platform for her. Maybe you can find your mother if she isn't dead," was the last thing Señor González said

---

[*] stupid

to her as she got onto the train.

As the train pulled into Retiro Station, Laura scanned the platform for a nun but didn't see one. She was determined to run away as fast as she could if she did.

My mother could barely take care of herself after my father died. That's why she took me to the orphanage. The nuns said going to the country was for my health. What lies! How can being beaten and working like a dog be healthy? And if I didn't get out of there, I'd have ended up flat on my back in some stable, producing kids and living in shit for the rest of my life, a servant to some cabrón. *And now they want to send me back to the nuns so I can do laundry and sew until my hands are as red and swollen as my mother's were. No! The last thing I'll do is go back to them. I will sing the tango in Buenos Aires, and everyone will listen.*

Inside the station, she felt as if she were in a church. Shafts of sunlight, giant columns that soared to towering arched ceilings, polished stone floors. Across the street, the clock in the Tower of the English struck three. In the café, women with perfect faces and elegant dresses sipped tea under chandeliers. The only dress she owned was the one she was wearing, and it smelled like cow shit.

She was going to be an actress and a singer, and perhaps she could find her mother. She knew they had lived on Defensa Street in San Telmo. Celia had circled it on the map and drawn the route from the station.

She left the station and walked along Avenida Viceroy Vértiz* past the Plaza San Martín, down Reconquista, across Corrientes and the Plaza de Mayo towards Independencia.

And when she reached Defensa, the only street name in Buenos Aires she could remember, she didn't recognize anything.

Laura knocked on the door of the house on Defensa where the man in the café on Chile Street said there might be rooms for rent and she should speak to the woman they called La Renga.

"*Hola*. Is anyone there?" She hammered harder on the door with her fist. Just as she was ready to give up, a boy of six or seven opened the door. His face was smudged with dirt and he was wearing a ragged shirt that was much too big for him – a man's shirt. The sleeves were rolled up, which made his skinny arms seem even thinner. He looked up at her without blinking.

"*Hola*. I'm looking for La Renga."

"Just a minute." The boy closed the door. A few minutes later, it opened slightly. A woman with eyes like black beads and stray strands of grey hair sprouting from her head in all directions eyed her suspiciously. The woman pulled her white lace shawl, yellowed with age, tighter around her shoulders.

---

* Renamed Avenida del Libertador in 1950.

"*Hola*, señora, I need to rent a room."

"Sorry, I have no rooms now." Just as La Renga was closing the door, Laura stopped it with her foot and pushed it open enough to squeeze herself inside.

"I'm only looking for a very small room. Even a closet will be OK. I really need a place to live."

"Sorry, there are no rooms here. Go home to your mother."

"I don't know where my mother is."

"Well, look what the dog dragged in." A man with thick grey hair, his face shiny with sweat, a cigarette dangling from his lower lip, was slouched in a chair against the wall to the right. He slapped his knee. "*Che, piba*, come over here. I might have a place for you to sleep in my room if you behave."

"Armando, leave her alone." La Renga hobbled in between Armando and Laura. A large, mangy grey dog, which was tied to the leg of a heavy wooden table, strained at its rope and snarled.

Laura scowled at Armando. "I came to talk to the señora, not you!"

"I've seen prettier, but you're not bad-looking." Armando put his *mate* on the ground, slithered off his chair, and swaggered across the patio, running his hands through his greasy hair and making an unsuccessful attempt to suck in his belly. He sauntered in a circle around them. "Let's have a look at you. Not much of a face, but in the dark, it's only the body that matters anyway." Laura stepped out of his way just in time to avoid a slap on the behind.

"Keep your comments and your hands to yourself, you old degenerate. Don't think just because I'm a girl, you can do what you like with me. If I choose to sell myself, I'll decide when and to whom."

Armando cleared his throat, spat, and raised his hand to strike. "You ungrateful little whore!"

"Armando!" La Renga stood in front of him. She was only about half his size and her head only came up to his shoulders. The dog snapped and growled, trying to shake its head free of the rope.

"I should knock your head off. And yours too, you old witch! Sleep on the street, then, stupid bitch, and don't come crying to me later when you have nowhere else to go."

Laura stood beside La Renga. "I'll go back to Magdalena and sleep with the cows before I do that."

Armando took a threatening step towards them. La Renga didn't move. The dog went crazy, barking and throwing itself against the table.

"Quiet, Perro!" La Renga yelled at the dog, which slunk back and lay down against the table leg, licking its front paws.

"Thank you, señora. I'll go now." Laura turned towards the door.

"Wait. I might…I might have a room." La Renga stood up very straight and smoothed her skirt. If you hadn't seen her walk, you wouldn't have known she had a bad leg. Armando scratched the back of his head, furious. La Renga ignored him and turned to Laura. "It's a very small room."

"I don't need much space. I don't have anything."

"I expect the rent to be paid once a week. Five pesos. In advance, exactly on time."

"I don't have money now, but I will next week."

"Just what I thought." La Renga crossed her arms.

"I will have it next week. I'm going to find a job tomorrow. I'm going to be a singer and an actress."

Armando cleared his throat, spat, crushed his cigarette butt with his heel, and shook a fist at the dog, which growled back at him. He lurched back to his chair and filled his *mate* with hot water from the kettle on the floor beside him.

La Renga shot a glance at him and took a deep breath. "I suppose I can make an exception this time, but don't push your luck. I expect the rent by the end of next week. You can try the Teatro Avenida. They're always looking for girls there."

"Bah!" Armando sucked noisily on his *mate*.

La Renga's eyes narrowed. "Or two weeks from now at the most."

"Oh, thank you, señora!" Laura threw her arms around La Renga and kissed her on the cheek.

"All right, all right." La Renga waved her away, looking flustered at the unexpected embrace. "Come back later – in two hours. The room's full of old things. I need to clear it out first."

"I can help you, señora."

"No, I'll do it myself." La Renga's hands were on her hips. "Just make sure you're back here in two hours, girl." She turned and lumbered away.

"I will! I promise. Oh, I forgot to tell you my name is Laura."

La Renga stopped and, without turning around, said, "I am…I am…Josefa. Pepa."

"Thank you, Doña Pepa!"

When Laura came back to the house that afternoon, as she followed La Renga across the patio, she could hear Armando yelling from a room at the back for something to eat, and she promised herself she'd kill him before she would be his servant. La Renga led her to a room on the second floor at the back, number 15.

"I've found you a blanket. And you can have those too." La Renga pointed to a dark-green dress and a pair of black leather shoes on the bed. "And these." She fumbled in her pocket and produced a pair of gold earrings and a black hair comb inlaid with pieces of shell. "You'll need some decent things to wear when you go for that job at the theatre."

"Oh, they're so beautiful!"

"I only want to make sure I get my rent next week. If you go to the theatre looking the way you do now, you'll never get the job and I won't get paid. Nobody's using that dress anymore. It looks about the right size. And you certainly can't wear the shoes you've got on, so you might as well have those."

"Thank you, Doña Pepa!"

"For what? There's no point just leaving that dress hanging on a hook, so you can have it. Now, I have things to do. Those miserable good-for-nothings have left me a pile of work downstairs, as usual." La Renga lumbered out into the hallway.

The room had only enough space for a narrow bed and small table. If Laura stretched out her arms, she could almost touch both walls at once. On the wall was a small oval mirror, which had a lot of dark spots where the backing had peeled off, so she couldn't see all of her face at the same time. But it was *her* room, the first one she'd ever had all to herself. No more of Luisa's whining. No more getting up in the dark to feed the cows. No more having to be nice to that *porquería,* Enrique, just because he was Señor González' precious son.

She tried on the dress. It was a little big, but not much. She was surprised at how light it felt when she put it on. The shoes were also a bit big, so, into the toes, she stuffed some of the newspaper that had been used to wrap her bread. Finally, she put on the earrings and slid the comb into her hair.

"You will get that job," she said to her reflection in

the mirror. "You will sing and they will listen." She could still smell cows, but, perhaps, when she wore this dress, no one else would notice.

That night, she lay in bed listening to the sounds of the house. A woman singing softly in an unfamiliar language. The shuffle of boots up and down the stairs and along the corridor. One door opening, another closing. A bottle smashing, Armando shouting. A heavy chair being dragged across the floor. Children squabbling. The dog barking. A man and a woman gasping for air, making love.

Laura waited her turn backstage at the Teatro Avenida with two other girls – Mirta, a tall, angular girl who said, at least three times, that her father was half-British, and Angelina, an Italian from La Boca who was squeezed into a grey dress that was at least a size too small.

"It's my sister's dress. She's very skinny. My mother let it out as much as possible, but it's still too tight on me." When Angelina's name was called, she walked stiffly onto the stage, as if she were afraid the seams would split, and stood very still.

"OK, girl, let's see what you can do," the director called from the front seats. Even from the other side of the stage, Laura could see Angelina's face turn bright-red. The director would certainly have seen it too. In a high, timorous voice, Angelina sang a song Laura didn't recognize. She looked tiny. Laura held her breath, hoping Angelina's seams wouldn't split and thinking that they could have switched dresses.

"OK, thank you, señorita. You can go." Angelina was only halfway through the second chorus when the director stopped her. She stumbled off the stage and stared at the floor as she mumbled a passing goodbye to Laura and Mirta.

Mirta was next. She smiled at the director, picked up the hem of her skirt just enough to show her legs, strode to the centre of the stage, and sang, "I am the dark-haired woman, the most graceful." Laura recognized Villoldo's tango about the ideal woman, happy at home in the country, faithful to her cowboy – "La Morocha." Humberto's father had taught it to the stable boys. They used to whistle the tune and pinch Luisa until she gave in and sang a couple of verses.

> "I am the dark-haired Argentinian woman,
> The one who does not feel regrets
> And spends her life happy
> With her songs.
>
> I am the gentle companion
> Of the noble *porteño gaucho.*[*]

---

[*] *Soy la morocha argentina / La que no siente pesares / Y alegre pasa la vida / Con sus cantares. / Soy la gentil compañera / Del noble gaucho porteño.*

The one who saves her affection
For her master."[*]

Laura wanted to spit. What did this stupid little *puta* with the half-British father know about the country? She should try living there with Enrique González and the rest of those noble *gauchos*. She wouldn't get much chance to save her affection for anyone with them grabbing at her. She'd be singing a different song after a week with them.

The director let Mirta finish the entire song. "Thank you, señorita. Please don't leave. I would like to talk to you after the auditions. Next."

Laura adjusted her dress, which suddenly felt three sizes bigger, took a deep breath, and stepped out onto the stage. If singing Villoldo would get her the job, she would give them Villoldo. The only other Villoldo tango she could think of was "El Choclo," the one he'd sung the day he visited the González' *estancia* – the one Celia had said was about things young girls shouldn't know.

She didn't look at the director and concentrated on the words she could remember, the music running through her head, and how light and soft the dress felt against her skin.

---

[*] *La que conserva la vida / Para su dueño.* (From the tango "La Morocha." 1905. Music: Enrique Saborido. Lyrics: Ángel Villoldo.)

And, just so she wouldn't forget how much she needed this job, she imagined Enrique González' stupid, fat face.

> "From a seed is born the plant
> That later gives us the corncob."[*]

She couldn't remember the rest of the verse, so she started the second one.

> "There are corncobs that have
> Heads of gold.
> Those are the ones I adore
> With tender passion."[†]

"OK, that's enough. You'll do. See me after the auditions."

Enrique González had finally been good for something.

Laura waited outside the director's office. Mirta had been in there for at least an hour. When she came out, her face was flushed and her hair needed combing. She looked distracted and cleared her throat.

"Señor De Rosa says that you are to go in now."

---

[*] *De un grano nace la planta / Que más tarde nos da el choclo.*
[†] *Hay choclos que tienen / Las espigas de oro. / Que son las que adoro / Con tierna pasión.* (From the tango "El Choclo." 1903. Music and lyrics: Ángel Villoldo.)

"OK, Morocha. See you later." Just as Laura was about to open the office door, she looked back over her shoulder. "But you'd better do up your top button before you go out into the street."

Señor De Rosa sat with one foot up on his massive wooden desk. He looked at her the way Armando had, but this time, she was alone and she needed this job. Again, it helped if she imagined Enrique's face.

"So, you want to be an actress."

"Yes."

"Sit down." He motioned to a chair in front of the desk. She sat on the edge of the seat, determined to look sure of herself. He stood up and walked around the desk. She waited until she could feel his breath on the top of her head and, at the moment his hand was inches from her shoulder, she stood up. The back of her head smacked him hard in the face and he staggered backwards. "Son of a bitch!"

"Oh, señor, I'm so sorry! Are you all right? My God!"

Blood was streaming out of his nose, all over his nice suit. His face was white. "Just get out, you stupid girl! Get out!" He held a handkerchief under his nose. "Be at the rehearsal tomorrow morning at eleven o'clock. And don't be late or you won't have a job. You're lucky it's too late to hire anyone else."

Laura knew she wasn't the best singer in the show, or

the prettiest, but she didn't expect so many boos and whistles from the audience, which guaranteed she wouldn't last more than one night in *The Virgins of Teres*.

After the performance, she was summoned to Señor De Rosa's office. She expected him to be there and tell her she was out of the show. Instead, she found Mirta, sitting calmly beside his desk, her thin legs sticking out of the bottom of a brand-new dress, sipping on a glass of champagne, looking like the Princess of Monaco.

"*Hola*, Morocha. I see you're taking advantage of all the comforts here."

"Don't be jealous, Laura."

"Jealous? Of what? Of the fact that you have to screw that piece of crap so you can sit in his office and drink champagne and keep your job in this stinking show? *The Virgins of Teres*, my ass."

"Shut your mouth, you foul-mouthed little whore!" Mirta picked up her glass and threw champagne in Laura's face.

"So, I'm a little whore. And just what are *you*, then?"

"I'm an actress with a job." Mirta handed her an envelope. "This is a week's pay. Señor De Rosa said to give it to you and tell you you're out of the show. He's too busy to bother with you himself. Now get out."

Laura stuffed the envelope in her pocket and walked out the stage door into the street. After she gave Doña Pepa the rent, there would be a little money left over for some *mate* and bread. And she'd had her first taste of champagne.

∞

"Well, here comes our chorus girl, La Niña Bonita, star of the Teatro Bataclán." El Dentista shot Laura a toothy grin and wiped his hands on his pants. "Are you still too good for us, Bonita? I hear you're dancing on tables now. Maybe you're not quite so choosy these days. How about giving the rest of us a look at your legs?" He took a quick step back, did a little spin and a bow, and beckoned her with a grimy finger.

"Go to the devil, Dentista. I'll never be that desperate."

"We'll see about that when they whistle you out of a few more theatres and you have no one to sing for but the cows."

La Renga pulled a wet shirt out of her laundry basket and shook it at him. "Shut your miserable mouth, Dentista, or I'll let the dog take another chunk out of you. At least the girl has a job, which is more than anyone can say for you, you worthless bag of garbage."

"Maybe you'd like to dance with me, Renga." El Dentista wiggled his skinny bottom. La Renga scowled and went back to hanging up the laundry.

"Here's someone who can dance with you,

Dentista." Manuel, the oldest of Los Gallegos, the three Spanish kids, pushed Tito forward, laughing.

"Go dance with him yourself, stupid." Tito pushed him away and Manuel lost his balance, knocking over one of his little brothers, who was, as usual, right behind him.

"Come on, Bonita." El Dentista picked up the basket of wet clothes and scuttled around.

"Come on, Bonita, dance with me." Tito paraded across the patio in a near-perfect imitation of El Dentista. He knelt in front of the dog, blowing kisses in its face. El Dentista dropped the laundry basket and tried to grab Tito, but when he got too close, the dog snarled a warning and El Dentista backed off.

"Dance with me, Perro." Tito blew more kisses at the dog. The Gallego kids hung onto one another, laughing so hard they were choking. Los Palitos, the two skinny brothers from number 99, sat on the stairs, clapping and whistling. Even La Renga couldn't keep a straight face.

The more they laughed and clapped, the better Tito's impersonations became. He stuck out his stomach and swaggered up to Laura, running his hands through his hair.

"*Che,* Bonita. How about a dance?"

"He's Armando!" The Gallego kids howled with laughter and pounded the floor with their fists. Laura had seen Tito do this kind of thing before – imitating

El Puño going up the stairs to La Chica's room, tilting an imaginary hat over his eyes and pulling an imaginary knife out of an imaginary sleeve. Mimicking La Rusa's attempts to balance one child on her hip while trying to stuff food into the mouth of the other. Walking around the house with his eyes closed when he thought no one was watching, pretending to be blind like El Ciego, counting the steps between the table on the patio and the stairs, feeling his way along the second-floor corridor.

Laura tilted her face upwards, nose in the air, and sang "You'll haaaave to speak to my boyfriend about thaaaat."

Tito sang back. "And whoooo's your boyfriend?" He scratched his belly, leaned back, and snorted, his hands on his hips. "He caaaaan't be as handsome as me."

"Much handsoooomerrrr."

"Oh yeah? What's his naaaame?"

"They call him Tiiiiiito."

Tito threw his head back and strolled across the patio, a hand in one pocket. Los Palitos nudged each other. Los Gallegos were rolling on the ground in hysterics. The dog barked and wagged its tail.

"Good show." The patio went silent, all eyes on Armando, who was slouched against the wall near the front door. No one had heard him come in. He applauded slowly, stumbled to the stairs, and sat down beside Los Palitos. No one moved. When he was drunk, he was unpredictable.

"Don't stop. I was enjoying it." Armando tried to stuff his shirt tails into his pants. His belly spilled out where he'd popped a button.

Tito broke the silence. "*Che, papusa.*"* He staggered in a slow drunken circle around the patio, sticking out his belly and combing his hair with his fingers. He dragged on an imaginary cigarette and raised his eyebrows at Laura, who crossed her arms and pretended to ignore him. Armando slapped his thigh and roared. It was obvious he had no idea it was himself he was laughing at.

The patio was stinking hot that afternoon and there was no breeze. Laura and Tito could hear Armando snoring in his room, probably sleeping off half a bottle of *ginebra*. La Renga had gone shopping. El Dentista had gotten bored with tormenting everyone and gone out to the racetrack. By some miracle, La Rusa's kids were both asleep. The dog was stretched out under the table.

"Too bad I can't take you to the club with me, Tito. You're good," Laura said. "That crowd won't be satisfied for long with the same songs night after night. Men write all the tangos, so I have to keep changing the words. If I want to keep the job, I'm going to have

---

* doll

to come up with some new songs."

"Why can't you take me to the club?"

"It's no place for a kid."

"I'm almost ten."

"Too young."

"Why don't you make up your own songs? I do."

"You make up songs, Tito?"

"Yeah, lots of them. I have one about that stupid guy, El Delicado. It's called 'Flaco, Fino, y Delicado.' He sits outside the bar on the corner, watching the girls when they come to buy vegetables from the Italian across the street. He thinks he's better than everyone, that he's perfect. Everyone laughs when I sing that one. Sometimes, El Puño and Gloria's friends even give me money."

"How does it go?"

Tito drew himself up to his full height, pursed his lips as if he had a foul smell under his nose, brushed his shoulder with his hand, and pranced around as if he were afraid of stepping in something.

"Slim, refined, and delicate,
Tough and upstanding.
Educated and on top of this,
With the look of a classy guy.
You think you're a Gengiskan
With airs of a great gentleman.
But you're only a clown
With shit in your heart

And an idiot with the women.
Skinny, weak, and stupid,
Born in ruins
With not even one penny for food."*

"Bravo!" Laura clapped her hands. "

"Everyone likes the part about Gengiskan," Tito said. "It's my favourite part."

"Who's Gengiskan?"

"He was the king of Mongolia nine hundred years ago. He had thousands of wives and everyone had to do what he told them to. I don't think El Delicado has even one wife, but he also thinks he can tell everyone what to do. El Dentista said Armando told him the stories about Gengiskan. Armando can read. Can you?"

"No. What about you?"

"Well, a bit. Mostly the numbers. El Dentista sometimes gives me money to go and pay the *quiniela* man for Armando's lottery tickets. Doña Pepa says I should go to school like the Gallego kids, but I don't have time right now. I have to work."

"What happened to your parents, Tito?"

---

* *Flaco, fino, y delicado, / Durito muy bien parado. / Educado y además, / Con apariencias de bacán. / Que te crees un Gengiskan / Con humos de gran señor. / Si solo sos un bufón / Con mierda en el corazón / Y salame con las minas. / Flaco, puto, y bobina, / Que nacistes en la ruina / Sin un mango pa' morfar.* (From the tango "Flaco, Fino, y Delicado." 1990. Oscar Casas.)

"Doña Pepa told me they died, so she took care of me when I was a baby. Now, I take care of myself." He kicked at a loose tile on the floor. "How about your parents, Laura?"

"My father died when I was a baby too. My mother couldn't take care of me, so I had to live in a place with nuns. When I was nine, I got sick, and they sent me to live in the country, in Magdalena."

"Were there animals there?"

"With the nuns or in the country?" Laura laughed.

"In the country!" Tito kicked at the tile again and it lifted away from the floor.

"Yes, lots of them."

"Why couldn't your mother take care of you?" Tito slid the tile back into place with his foot and stamped it down.

"I don't know."

"Is she dead too?"

"I don't know. Maybe."

"Didn't the nuns teach you to read?"

"No. We girls only learned how to sew and do laundry."

"*Che*, Tito." They heard the slow shuffle of slippers along the corridor upstairs.

"*Hola,* señor," Tito called back. He whispered in Laura's ear, "Señor Esteban. He can't see, so they call him El Ciego. But Doña Pepa says I should use his real name because that's more polite. He's coming down to wait for La Chica. He likes her a lot. She went out this morning and, even though he's blind, he always knows when she goes out and comes back. El Puño beats her if she's not here when he comes. She sometimes has bruises and once she had a black eye."

"Why does she let El Puño beat her?"

"I don't know." Tito shrugged and rubbed his nose with the palm of his hand. "I can teach you my song and you can sing it in the club if you want to."

"Thank you, Tito. It's a good song."

They watched Esteban descend the stairs, carrying his *mate* and *bombilla*.*

"Eighteen steps," Tito whispered to himself. He walked over to the table. "Do you want to drink some *mate*, Señor Esteban?"

"Yes, good. Thank you, Tito." Esteban walked slowly but surely to the stool beside the wooden table to which the dog was tied and sat down. The dog flicked its tail and panted but didn't get up.

Esteban was wearing a shirt that Laura had seen Doña Pepa hang to dry – a clean white one. His face was shaven and his thinning grey hair was combed back. He wasn't young, but he certainly didn't look as old as El Dentista or Doña Pepa.

Tito carefully filled the *mate* with *yerba*† from a tin on the shelf above the table and poured in hot water. He

---

* metal straw used for drinking *mate*
† *mate* tea leaves

101

sucked on the *bombilla,* spat the first bitter mouthful at the ground, added more water, and then handed the *mate* to Esteban.

"Would you like to drink some *mate* with us, señorita*?*" Esteban turned his head to face Laura, making her feel as if he could see her. She pulled a stool over to the table and sat down. The three of them passed the *mate* back and forth, waiting for La Chica, hoping she would come back before El Puño returned.

Laura swore to herself she would never let any man beat her again. *Maybe all I'm good for now is the chorus line and singing in dives, but let those stupid men think what they want about me and make idiots of themselves over a pair of legs if it gets me what I want. All I know is I have to make enough money so I won't have to take more beatings from anyone or spend my whole life on my back under some* cabrón, *like that poor girl of El Puño's.*

The pianist played the first few chords of "El Choclo." Laura waited for the violin and the steady beat of the *bandoneón* and then walked out onto what they called the stage, which was actually just a raised wooden platform. Only one step separated her from the floor, where the audience sat at small tables, smoking and downing grappa*, ginebra*, whiskey, wine, and champagne

"*Che, pebeta*, let's see what you've got." The skinny man at one of the front tables threw back a mouthful of grappa straight from the bottle and slapped the shoulder of the fat man beside him. They always sat at that table, steadily getting drunk, grinning at each other and leaning back in their chairs, leering at the girls.

The rest of the audience joined in. "*Che, mina.* Come on! Give us a song!"

"And give us a look at those legs!" The fat man leaned so far forward that his chair slid out from under him and he landed on the floor. Whistles and hoots. It was all Laura could do to stop herself from walking over to their table and pouring grappa over both their heads.

But all of a sudden, she could smell cows. And when the fat man struggled back into his seat, from that angle, he looked, just for a moment, like Enrique González.

She stood at the edge of the platform, motioned to the orchestra to stop playing, and waited for the audience to settle down. She slid one hand back over the side of her face, caressing the comb in her hair. Her fingers slipped down to the base of her neck and over her chest and picked up the hem of her dress, finally coming to rest on her hip. La Bonita threw her head back, tilted it to one side, looked straight at the skinny man at the front, and sang without the orchestra. "*Flaco, fino, y delicado, durito muy bien parado*."

The skinny man grinned, and his stare burned into her body.

"Refined, upstanding! Gustavo, I think she likes you," someone yelled from the back.

"She wants you, *hermano.*" The fat man laughed and punched Gustavo in the shoulder. There were shouts and howls from all over the room. She watched Gustavo's expression change as she sang the next lines.

"Educated and on top of this,
With the look of a classy guy.
You think you're a Gengiskan
With airs of a great gentleman."

"*Che,* Gengiskan, save some for the rest of us."

Laura turned her back on all of them, hand on her hip, face to the ceiling.

"But you're only a clown
With shit in your heart
And an idiot with the women.
Skinny, weak, and stupid,
Born in ruins,
With not even one penny for food.*"*

The fat man doubled over laughing and sprayed a mouthful of grappa all over his shirt. Fists pounded on tables. "A clown with shit in your heart! Did you hear that one, Gustavo?"

"An idiot with the girls!"

"Che, Gustavo! How did you like that? Skinny, weak, and stupid."

"Shut up and drink, Diego. More likely it's about you, you stupid shit."

Shouts from the back. "Quiet! I want to hear the rest of this!"

"Yeah, shut your mouths up there so we can hear too!"

Laura walked slowly to the piano and leaned against it. She scanned her audience and waited until she was sure every man could feel her eyes on him. The piano player picked up on the tune, and soon she heard the first notes from the *bandoneón.* When the room was absolutely still, she improvised a new verse for Tito's tango. As she sang, she wasn't sure where the words were coming from.

> "Today I tell you, *cabrón,*
> Hold on to this tango.
> You aren't worth one penny.
> And you make yourself bitter.
> You're only a moron.
> And with your fish face,
> I have no pity for you."[*]

---

[*] *Hoy te digo, che cabrón, / Agárrate de este tango. / Que así no valés un mango. / Y te hacés el amargado. / Si solo sos un tarado. / Y con tu cara de pescado, / A mí ni pena me das.* (From the tango "Flaco, Fino, y Delicado." 1990. Oscar Casas.)

She strutted across the stage, singing directly to each of them in turn, making sure she didn't miss one of them. The fat guy who looked like Enrique cheered. Everyone clapped. And she knew that every single man in the audience imagined that La Bonita was not singing about him but about some other man in the room.

The next night, as soon as Laura walked onto the stage, a man yelled from one of the back tables, "*Che, piba*, sing "Flaco, Fino, y Delicado!" People whistled and pounded on the tabletops. The pianist nodded to the *bandoneón* player, and Laura waited for silence. As she sang the first lines, she closed her eyes and could see Tito swaggering around the patio, imitating Armando and singing the new lines they'd just made up that afternoon.

She would have money for Doña Pepa that week.

EL LOCO

"Everyone said that he was crazy. That's why they called him El Loco. Maybe he was crazy, but I think that he was also very intelligent. He taught me how to read. He knew all about the stars and faraway places, and he could speak many languages."

∞

El Loco was talking to the dog. Not just go, sit, come, but a real conversation. And the dog was answering. Not just a whimper, or a growl, or a whine, but a combination of all these and other sounds that had no human names.

Tito watched from the shadows in the corner of the patio.

El Loco could talk to everyone and everything. He had many voices, spoke many languages. When he asked the ants to stop running across La Renga's table, they stopped. During his long conversations with La Rusa in a language no one else understood, her kids were unusually quiet. He was the only one who could find the way through Gloria's craziness and make her laugh.

El Loco was also reading from the book he was holding in a language Tito didn't recognize. The dog sniffed and sighed and rested its chin on its paws. El Loco grinned.

"Yes, that's it. That's it, Perro!" He rubbed the dog between the ears. The dog thumped its tail on the ground and panted.

Everyone had a different story about El Loco. He was the son of a rich family. He had no family. He had killed his wife, no, it was his uncle, no, his father. Someone had tried to kill him. He was Spanish, Italian, Russian, a Turk. A teacher, a magician, a thief. He was actually a woman. He didn't need to eat or sleep. Once, he had fallen asleep for three years, and when he woke up, he couldn't remember his name. Sometimes he looked old and, other times, no more than twenty. Some people said he'd started most of the stories himself. It was possible to believe anything about him.

El Loco walked to the centre of the patio and looked up at the tree. He always faced the same direction and stared at exactly the same spot, night after night. His long green jacket, too heavy for that time of year, hung from his thin body. His hair stuck out from under a black bowl of a hat, and a long, frayed multicoloured scarf was wound twice around his neck.

His shoelaces had been broken and knotted back together. He looks like a clown, Tito thought.

El Loco would stand there like that for hours. He would close his eyes and was still for so long you could almost imagine he'd stopped breathing.

Tito crept across the patio. Yes, El Loco's eyes were closed. In the moonlight, you could imagine his face was carved from stone and he was not alive, only a statue of a blind clown.

Tito felt a sudden urge to sneeze. Just when he knew he couldn't hold it back any longer, one of the statue's eyes flicked open, making Tito jump and sneeze at the same time. His other eye opened before Tito could run away.

"Perhaps you're catching a cold," El Loco said.

Tito dragged the back of his hand across his nose. "Why do you always stand there and stare at the tree like that?"

"I don't look at the tree. I look at the sky. I can see the stars through the leaves."

"But you can see the stars from anywhere on the patio, or you can go out to the Plaza Dorrego. Doña Pepa and I go there and sit on the bench sometimes. Why do you always have to look through the leaves to see the stars?

"Ask the dog," El Loco said.

"Ask the dog? That's crazy!"

"You're right. He doesn't know everything. It might

be better to ask the ants."

"You can't talk to ants!"

"Then what was I doing today?"

Tito sniffed and rubbed his nose. "Everybody says you're crazy, just like Doña Gloria."

"Is that what they say?"

"Yes. Are you?"

"Am I what?"

"Crazy."

"Am I?"

"That's what I asked you. I don't know."

"Neither do I," El Loco said. "I'll ask the ants later."

Tito frowned and stared at El Loco's book. El Loco held it out to him. Tito shook his head. "I can't read. Well, I can a little – the numbers zero and one. And the letter O is easy because it looks just like zero. I also know T." He made a T with his forefingers. "And this is X." He crossed them to form an X.

El Loco nodded. "That's a good start. T is half your name, and O is in the other half. X is very useful and so are the numbers. There aren't even thirty more letters. It shouldn't take long to learn the rest of them."

"How long?"

"That depends on you and the letters. We can start now."

"Now?"

"It's either now or yesterday or tomorrow. Yesterday takes some time to master. Tomorrow may not come. That only leaves now."

"OK."

"Tell me about the stars in the Plaza Dorrego."

"I thought you were going to teach me how to read."

"That's what I'm doing," El Loco said. "Here, hold this for a minute." He handed the book to Tito.

"It's heavy."

"The longer you hold it, the heavier it gets. It's the weight of the words."

"What's the book about?"

"I'm not sure."

"But you were reading it just now."

El Loco nodded.

"You were reading it to the dog."

"Yes. He's a good listener. Give me the book back and tell me about the stars in the Plaza Dorrego."

"They look like the stars you can see from here."

"So, why do you have to go to the Plaza Dorrego to see them?"

"Because Doña Pepa likes to sit on the bench there. In the summer, it's cooler there than here on the patio, and quieter too."

"Ah, so the stars are different out there."

Tito rubbed his nose. "She says that every time a person dies, they become part of a star. Like her mother. And my mother."

"Which one is your mother's star?"

Tito pointed upwards. "It's that one. There. That really bright one. It's almost the brightest one in the whole sky."

"Canopus," El Loco said.

"What?"

"Canopus, the pilot."

"What?"

"In Carina, the keel."

"What's a keel?"

"Part of the ship."

"What ship?"

"I'll tell you later. It isn't important now."

"Why not?"

"Because now you want to learn to read."

"How do you know so much about the stars?"

"Because I look at them every night and I've learned a lot from my friends. The dog knows a lot too."

Tito frowned. "How do your friends know so much about the stars?"

"Because they look at them as much as I do."

"Do they look at them through trees too?"

"Sometimes."

"So, where are your friends?"

"In a place where the stars are upside down."

"Hah! You *are* crazy."

"Maybe. But whether I am or not doesn't change the fact that the stars are upside down there and the moon is backwards, and when it's summer here, it's winter there."

Tito shook his head, rolled his eyes, and crossed his arms.

"Ask the dog if you don't believe me. See that star?" El Loco pointed to the sky. "The brightest one. It's called Sirius, the Dog Star. You can see it from here and from the place where my friends live. It looks brighter than your mother's star but only because it's much closer. Your mother's star is very far away. You can only see it from here, not from where my friends live."

"So, they must live very far from here."

"Yes, very far but very close."

"That doesn't make sense."

"No, no sense at all."

"How far away is my mother's star?"

"Much farther than the Dog Star. It looks small because it's so far away, but it's very big."

"How big?"

"Much bigger than the sun. Do you want to learn to read now?"

Tito shrugged. "OK."

"We'll start with L. It's the first letter of *loco*." El Loco dug in the pocket of his jacket and pulled out a pencil and a scrap of paper. He sat on the patio floor, put the paper in front of him and smoothed the creases, and then handed the pencil to Tito.

"You said you know how to write a T."

Tito nodded and sat down across from El Loco.

"Write a T, but upside down."

"Upside down? Why?"

"So I can see it right side up from where I am."

After Tito had written the upside-down T, El Loco fished in his pocket and produced an eraser. Tito watched him rub out half of the top (now at the bottom) of the upside-down T.

"There, that's an L. Now write an O. You don't have to change anything for me this time because, even when you're upside down, nothing is still nothing."

Tito carefully drew an O.

"Now write another O." After Tito had done that, El Loco rubbed out part of one side of the O. "Take a little away from nothing and you get something. That's a C. Now write another O. There. A little more nothing and you have a word!"

"That's a real word?"

"Yes. *loco*."

Tito stared at the word. "How do I write my name?"

"Well, you can already write most of it. You only need one more thing." El Loco edged himself over beside Tito.

"I will watch you write your name from your side. Write a T. Now, write the number one. There, yes! Now another T. And now an O. That's it!"

"That's it? That's my name?"

"Yes, unless your name isn't Tito. I'll ask the dog to make sure it is." El Loco walked over to the sleeping dog and whispered into its face. The dog let out a sigh.

El Loco nodded. "Yes, he says it is. So now you know how to write your name."

"Show me more letters."

"Later. Now it's time to go out to the Plaza Dorrego and look at the stars."

The walk to the Plaza Dorrego took much longer with El Loco than it had with anyone else, even Doña Pepa. El Loco went a few steps and then stopped to look up at the sky. He walked backwards, around lampposts, up and down curbs. He hummed to himself and smiled at everyone they passed.

When they finally reached the bench in the square, Tito sat down, but El Loco walked around the bench twice, once again backwards, and finally, sat on the ground in front of it.

"Why are you sitting on the ground?"

"Why are you sitting on the bench?"

"That's a stupid question. Everyone sits on the bench."

"If everyone sits on the bench, there must be a reason. Why are you sitting on the bench?"

Tito sighed.

"All right, we'll worry about that later. I can see your mother's star very well from here."

Tito nodded. "Is it really bigger than the sun?"

"Canopus? Yes, much bigger."

"You still haven't told me what Canopus is."

"There is a story that Canopus was the pilot of a ship that belonged to a king of Greece, and when Canopus died, he and the ship became stars. And there are other stories of sailors travelling through seas with floating rocks that could crash together and grind ships into millions of tiny pieces."

"Where's Greece?"

"On the other side of the world, where the stars are upside down."

"How could Canopus become a star?"

"How could your mother become a star? Look closely at this." El Loco took off his hat. Hundreds of tiny white stitches had been sewn into the black material. Tito had noticed the odd pattern on El Loco's hat before but hadn't thought much about it. "This is the sky from here. This is your mother's star." El Loco pointed to a stitch that was larger than all of the others, except for one. "And that's the Dog Star, the brightest of all."

Tito stared at the hat, at the sky, and then back at the hat.

"This is my summer hat here," El Loco said. "I have another one for winter."

"Who sewed all those stars on your hat?"

"I did. I'm not quite finished yet, but it's a good start."

"The inside of your hat has stars too."

"Yes, but not the same ones." El Loco turned the hat inside out. "These are the stars in the place where everything is upside down and backwards. It's winter there now. Look at the sky. Look at the inside of the hat. The stars are not the same at all."

"Where's my mother's star?"

"Remember, they can't see your mother's star there. You can only see it here."

Tito ran his fingers over the stars on El Loco's hat.

"That place must be really far away."

"That depends on many things," El Loco said.

Tito woke up early the next morning. Even La Renga was still asleep. He tiptoed past her bed, closed the door quietly behind him, and went out onto the patio.

He dragged a chair over to the table and sat down. He felt in his pocket for the pencil El Loco had given him and carefully unfolded the piece of paper with his words.

LOCO

TITO

He moved the letters around, inventing new words.

TOCO OCTI

Then he remembered that, in the signs on the street, not all words had the same number of letters.

T N O   T I   I T C O I

"What are you doing?" Manuel, the oldest of the Gallego kids, peered over his shoulder.

"Nothing."

"Doesn't look like nothing to me."

"I'm writing."

"Writing? You can write?"

"A little."

"Let me see." Manuel grabbed the piece of paper. "What does it say?"

"That's my name there. Tito. And that says *loco*. Look." Tito pointed to each letter. "L O C O."

Manuel waved the piece of paper above his head, chanting, "Titoloco, titoloco."

"Give it to me, Manuel!" Manuel was taller than Tito. To get his words back, he'd have to take Manuel down. He leaped up on the chair and lunged at Manuel, and they both landed hard on the ground, Tito on top.

The dog, which had been sleeping under the table, barked and La Rusa's children started to cry. The other two Gallego kids, Manuel's little brothers, always excited by a fight, crept onto the patio and watched from beside the stairs, punching their fists into the air.

Manuel flailed his arms around. By inching his way up Manuel's body, Tito managed to grab the piece of paper, but Manuel clenched it even tighter and wriggled out from under Tito, who fell backwards with only half of it in his hand.

O

I T O

O C T I

I T C O I

"Manuel, you miserable little rat, look what you've done! My words!" Tito ran at Manuel, fists pounding. Manuel put his hands over his face to avoid the blows and dropped the other half of the piece of paper.

Armando shouted from his room. "Shut that racket up or I'll come out and knock your heads off! Can't a man even get a few decent hours of sleep in his own house?"

"Manuel, Tito, stop it! Perro, shut up." La Renga, still in her nightdress, stood in the doorway of her room. "All of you, stop it now!" Manuel's brothers slunk back into their room.

"OK, OK, I don't want your stupid paper or your stupid words! Get off me!" Manuel rolled away from Tito, stumbled to the front door without looking at La Renga, and ran out into the street. La Renga scowled in his direction and went back into her room, closing the door behind her.

Tito pushed himself to his feet and picked up the other half of his words.

L O C
T
T O C O
T N O T I

He sat down at the table and tried to line the two halves up.

"Good morning." Tito jumped. El Loco was standing right behind him. "What are you doing?"

"The paper is torn." Tito smacked his fist on the table. "Right in the middle of my words!"

"Perhaps there's another solution to this problem."

"What?"

"Instead of trying to put the old words back together, you could write new ones."

"I don't know how."

"So, you must learn. That way, you'll never have to be afraid of anyone destroying what you've written because you know you can write more. Any time you need more words, come and find me so we can look for them together."

Tito lay in his bed in the corner of La Renga's room,

his head spinning with letters and stars. He felt under his pillow for the tear in the mattress cover, where he kept the small piece of glass with one rough edge that La Renga had found near the bench in the Plaza Dorrego one night they were out there looking at the stars. Some nights, before he went to sleep, he would trace its edges with his fingers, imagining it was a piece of his mother's star.

"Please stop fidgeting and go to sleep, Tito. You're keeping me awake."

"Doña Pepa, tell me about my mother."

La Renga sighed. "It's late, Tito. I've told you that story at least a hundred times."

"I want to hear it again, and then I promise I'll go to sleep."

"All right. She was pretty."

"Very pretty?"

"Yes, with beautiful, long hair."

"And the loveliest voice."

"Yes."

"The voice of an angel, no?"

"Yes, the voice of an angel."

"And she used to sing to me."

"Yes."

"So I would fall asleep."

"Yes. By the way, what were you and Manuel fighting about today?"

"He took something of mine and I was trying to get it back."

"What was it?'

"Some words."

"Words?"

"Yes. On some paper. I wrote them. El Loco showed me how."

"Oh?"

"I can write my name."

"That's good."

"Doña Pepa."

"Yes, Tito?"

"What was my mother's name?"

La Renga was quiet for a few seconds. "Carolina. Carolina Torres. I've also told you that more than a hundred times. Perhaps El Loco can show you how to write it."

Tito waited until he was sure La Renga was asleep and then slipped quietly out of the room. As he climbed the stairs, he craned his neck to look at the sky. It was a clear, still night, so it was easy to see the stars. He walked along the corridor on the second floor. As he passed Gloria's room, he could hear her muttering. "He is an honourable man."

Past La Chica's room. El Puño's growl cut through the wall like a knife. Past the silence of El Ciego's room to the end of the corridor, room 22. The door was open, just a crack. He stood there for a few seconds, listening, trying to decide what to do.

"Have you come looking for words?" El Loco's voice made him jump.

"How did you know I was here?"

"How did you know *I* was here? Come in. You might find what you're looking for in here."

Tito pushed the door open. The room had no furniture except a narrow bed along one wall and a low bench in the centre, on which were three books, some pieces of paper, and a small, burning candle. Long, quivering shadows played on the walls. El Loco's black hats hung on a hook inside the door. He was kneeling on the floor and writing, using the bench as a table. The piece of paper was filled with lines of numbers and letters. Tito recognized some of them.

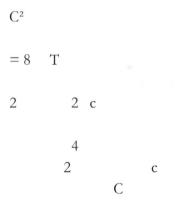

El Loco pushed the pieces of paper aside and put one of the books in front of Tito.

"See if any of the words you're looking for are in there."

Tito opened the book and scanned the clusters of letters. He recognized a few T's, C's, some O's. Each page had numbers in the top corner.

"Choose a word," El Loco said.

"That one. The one you wrote there, at the bottom of the page."

"*El*, e and l. Good idea to start with a short one."

"That's an L? It looks like the number one. Why does it look different from the L in *loco*?"

"Maybe for the same reason that O is sometimes nothing."

"Teach me how to write Carolina."

"OK. You already have half the letters you need. And this book is for you. You'll need it when you can read and write more words and when you want to learn more about the stars."

Soon, Tito's pockets were filled with words, collected from above shops and cafés, from street signs, from wagons carrying milk or vegetables, from the newspaper kiosk on Chile Street. Every night, he emptied his pockets, and he and El Loco knelt amid flickering shadows thrown by candlelight or sat under the stars in the Plaza Dorrego, scraps of paper spread out before them, spinning Tito's words into stories — stories of ships in the sky, of places where everything was upside down, and of stars that shone brighter than all the rest.

LA RUSA

"La Rusa means the Russian girl. That's what everyone called her, but El Loco told me that she wasn't really Russian. I'm not sure where she was from. Only El Loco could speak her language. He was the one who brought her to the house. He told me that her name was Marina. Some people thought that she could see the future. She had two kids. One of them, her daughter, had a bad foot, like Doña Pepa."

∞

Marina had never seen her mother's country, where men cut off the ears of people they called gypsies. After she'd buried her mother and burned the clothes and the blanket that had covered her mother as the fever shook her body, Marina walked for almost three days, carrying two-year-old Iva from San Nicolás to Buenos Aires, and collapsed outside the church on Venezuela Street. The nuns took her in, and Marek, who would never know his father, was born there.

She knew her son would grow up to be stronger than Zivan. She remembered how she'd once thought Marek had his father's eyes. But the face of her husband, whose body had been found floating in the Paraná River one morning, three days after he disappeared, was growing harder and harder to remember. She was losing the shape of his mouth, the curls of his thick dark hair, his voice, the touch of his hands, his songs, and the way he'd looked at her when they first met.

Iva's good foot pressed into the small of Marina's back and Marek released his grip on his mother's finger. He stopped sucking and his head rolled back against her arm. Marina whispered into his ear the secret name she'd given him to protect him against the devil. She did the same for her daughter. Iva would need protection. She'd had no talisman to protect her when she was born, and La Bruja's curse had left her with a twisted foot. But Marina knew that Iva's foot was the reason La Renga had given them this room.

El Loco had found them begging outside Retiro Station when Marek was only a month old. He had given her a few coins and, in the language of her mother, she whispered him a secret in exchange. He had come back the next day and taken Marina and the children to La Renga, who eyed Iva's twisted foot, sighed, and led them to the room beside El Loco's on the second floor.

Marina breathed in and out in time with her children. In moments like this, she could almost forget the hunger biting into her belly and the worry about what they would eat the next day. She slid Marek onto the bed, settled him beside his sister, lay down beside them, and tried to sleep. It was too hot to have her door completely closed. She could hear the dog barking and La Renga clattering about in the kitchen downstairs.

She blessed El Loco for his coins and for bringing her to this house, La Renga for the room and the bed, and even that brute, Armando, who, thanks to Iva and Marek, was not interested in her. La Renga should have had babies. That might have stopped Armando from treating her the way he did. She prayed for La Chica, that poor girl of El Puño's. And finally, she thanked God for making her Roma.

"He is an honourable man. He will marry me soon." Marina could hear Gloria, descending the stairs in a trance. The images of the future were always so clear – her mother's face, cold and white; the three fishermen pulling Zivan's body from the river; Gloria lying at the bottom of the stairs; La Chica's thin, broken body with the imprint of El Puño's fist on the side of her face; El Loco leaving one night in a snowstorm. She knew more visions would come. There would be no surprises, nothing unexpected. As a very young girl, she had seen herself with her two children on this bed, whispering their secret names. Her mother had told her these visions were a gift possessed by some of the women in the family.

"Pssst, Marina, I have something for the babies." She got up and crept to the door. El Loco held out his hand and she took the coins. Besides her children's breathing, El Loco's voice was the only thing that calmed her. He spoke in the language of her childhood and of things no one else did – how the moon would pass in front of the sun, and, in that half-light, you would be able to see the stars in the middle of the day. After that, the world would never be the same again.

Marina knotted the coins into the scarf around her waist and sat with El Loco on the sill in her doorway. They could see Gloria in her chair under the tree downstairs on the patio, arranging herself, waiting for Señor Rodríguez, who would never come, or for the men with their women and their music. Gloria was wearing the same blue dress as always and her long legs were showing. She was looking at herself in a small mirror, smoothing her hair and putting on lipstick.

"Tell me something," El Loco said.

"You will leave. It will snow that day."

A fist thumped on the front door. Gloria opened it and El Puño strode in, followed by three men – one carrying a guitar, one swinging a bottle, and a third one staggering behind them, already drunk and unsteady on his feet.

The man with the guitar was very young, not much more than a boy. Gloria ran her hand across the back of his neck, pulled off his cap, and put it on her head. He began to play and she swayed around him. The man with the bottle sauntered towards her in time to the music. They circled one another, every circle tighter until their bodies wound around one another. The drunk man tried to cut in but was pushed away and fell backwards. The man with the guitar played faster.

"It will snow and Gloria will slip on the stairs and fall. There will be blood. But you will already be gone," Marina said.

The men dragged chairs to the centre of the patio and sat down. El Puño went up the stairs. The man with the bottle got some cups from the kitchen and poured each of them a drink, which they tossed down their throats.

"After Gloria falls, she will sleep for many days and never wake up. She will die before her mother."

El Puño came along the corridor and turned down the stairs, pulling La Chica behind him. Marina had seen this many times before. La Chica would be passed to one of the men and dance with him until he was too drunk to dance anymore, and then he would follow her upstairs to her room. Gloria would dance with whomever was left. Later, the man would stagger down the stairs from La Chica's room, and another man who wasn't too drunk to climb the stairs would go up and take his turn with La Chica. The next morning, La Renga would be sweeping and cursing, saying this house was no better than a brothel.

"Tell me again about the river near your home in San Nicolás," El Loco said.

"The Arroyo del Medio is a little river. It told me stories, whispered secrets. When I was a child, I used to lie down beside it and just listen. It told me many things – that I would leave San Nicolás one day; that I would have two babies and live in this house. My mother said that after the men cut off her ear, she couldn't hear what the river in her country was saying anymore. That was before she came on the boat to Argentina. My mother's country is very far from here, in the place where you say the stars are upside down."

El Loco closed his eyes.

"She told me to use the gift she had lost. She said all the rivers run into one another and, no matter where I was, I would be able to hear the secrets carried by all of them. But she said that here the deep, dark rivers can swallow the secrets of all the little ones. And she was right. The secrets must be very far beneath the surface because sometimes I cannot hear anything."

They watched the man with the bottle follow La Chica up the stairs.

"La Chica will also fall, but it will not be an accident.

"When you arrive at the place you're going to, the sun will be only a ring of light. The sky will be dark even though it's daytime, so you'll be able to see the stars. You won't understand the language of the people around you. You will find something you've been searching for, for a long time."

"And after that?"

"I cannot see more."

"Perhaps that's better."

"Except for one thing. Sometimes I can see Tito with a little girl beside a river in a place where the moon is backwards and the stars are upside down."

∞

One morning in June, Tito was woken up, shivering, by the noise of the Gallego kids shouting out on the patio. It had been very cold for days and he'd been sleeping in his clothes, his blanket too thin to keep him warm. La Renga's bed was already empty. She always got up early to make breakfast for Dolores.

He got up and went out to the patio. The tiles were wet and big snowflakes were falling.

"Snow! I can't believe it! It's snowing. Just like in the pictures in the books at school!" The Gallegos were running around and yelling, sliding on the wet tiles. Armando staggered out of his room, rubbing his eyes. El Dentista was kicking snow into the dog's face.

Tito ran up the stairs to El Loco's room. The door was slightly open, but the room was empty. El Loco, his hats, and his books were gone.

The day after the snowfall, La Renga got up early, as usual, to make breakfast for Dolores and found Gloria in her nightdress, sprawled at the bottom of the stairs. After her sleepwalking episodes, which had become more and more frequent, Gloria wouldn't always return to her room, which used to be the library when Señor Rodríguez and his family lived there. In the mornings, she would sometimes be found lying on the patio or slumped, asleep, in a chair. La Renga would call Manuel and Tito to come and help carry Gloria back up to her room. La Renga would hoist her up by wedging her arms into Gloria's armpits and the boys took one leg each.

But this time, when they turned Gloria onto her back to carry her up the stairs, they saw a deep gash on her forehead and a dark-red stain in the snow where her head had been. The three of them managed to drag her upstairs and onto her bed.

Gloria's nightdress was wet and it was the only one she had. After dismissing the boys and closing the door, La Renga pulled off Gloria's nightdress and took out the blue dress from Señor Rodríguez. It was now too big for Gloria and slipped easily over her head. The colour had faded and it had been repaired and altered many times over the years. She gently settled Gloria into bed and covered her with a blanket. Then she went down to the kitchen and heated some water. She carried the kettle up the stairs and washed the blood off Gloria's face. *Señor Rodríguez gave her that dress more than forty years ago when Esteban was just a little boy. She is so thin now. So much blood, but not one mark on those long, beautiful legs.*

Over the next three days, Gloria would call, "Esteban, *mi amor?* Where are you, Esteban?" El Ciego sat in the chair by her bed, waiting for the moments his mother would wake up so he could help her sip some soup that La Renga had made. La Renga knew that the Esteban Gloria was calling for was not her son but his father. She also had thoughts she knew she shouldn't have. *Perhaps it would be better for all of us if, the next time she falls asleep, she doesn't wake up.*

It had been months since Gloria and Dolores had spoken to one another. Whenever they passed each other on the patio, Dolores would shake her head, muttering, "You have brought us so much shame," and Gloria would ignore her mother. After Gloria died, Dolores closed the door of her room and never came out again.

THE DEAD WHO SPEAK

The past will find us. After years of my not asking questions so my mother wouldn't cry, Argentina came looking for me.

When I was very young, my parents would sometimes stop talking and switch from Spanish to English when I came into the room, and I caught fragments of conversations I knew I wasn't supposed to hear – *tortura, policía, desaparecidos, las madres, azucena, plaza de mayo.* Words that solidified into weights I had to carry around. Names that hung like ghosts in every room in our house. *We should talk to Ale soon.*

In 1986, when I was nine, there were five movies nominated for the Academy Award for Best Foreign Film, including one from Argentina, *The Official Story.* On Oscar night, I was curled up on the couch beside Lito and my parents were sitting in the armchairs. Robin Williams, whom I knew as Popeye and Mork, was one of the hosts, but I lost interest during the long speeches. Lito said he didn't understand half of what they were saying and didn't believe the other half.

My mother looked over at him and put her finger to her lips. "Papá, *The Official Story* is the movie that Julián and I saw at the Toronto Film Festival last year. It's nominated for best foreign film. Do you remember I told you about that one and the other one from Argentina – *Las Madres*? It's nominated for best documentary. Shhhh! Listen. They're going to make the announcement about who won."

Again, I wondered who *Las Madres* were. My mother was leaning forward, her body tense, hands clenched, eyes riveted on the TV screen. My father had even closed his book, so I knew this must be something important. Lito closed his eyes and sipped his *mate*. I felt as if our living room were holding its breath.

The Argentinian film won and the director gave his speech, talking about a nightmare that had happened in Argentina. That was when I realized that, whether or not I asked my mother questions, she would cry anyway. I decided to stop asking, but I needed to know what the nightmare was.

I found the *Toronto Star* on the kitchen table the next day, open at the *Entertainment* section to an article on the Oscar winners. It said that *The Official Story* was a about a woman who finds out that her adopted daughter was taken by the government from a woman who was a political prisoner in Argentina.

I felt as if the newspaper had bunched itself into a fist and punched me in the stomach. If my parents had stayed in Argentina, I could have been stolen and given to another family.

Every evening after that, when I was sure my parents had finished with the newspaper, I'd take it up to my room and search the pages for news on Argentina. Everything I found felt like a small victory against the silence that surrounded me and seeped into my dreams, where it transformed itself into things that woke me. If I didn't do something, that silence would swallow me up, so I wrote everything down in a notebook that I kept in my schoolbag and carried it around with me everywhere.

Some words in the newspaper articles were unfamiliar and loaded with dread. The *Oxford English Dictionary* became my ally. I added the words to my notebook and would repeat them over and over again, letting them settle, take shape. *Abduction – taking a person away by force. Illegally taking a child from parents or guardians.*

If I heard anyone coming up the stairs, I would slam the dictionary shut and flip to the comics.

I finally found out who *Las Madres* were. A couple of months after the Oscars, I read an article by Michele Landsberg about Renée Epelbaum, whose three children, Luis, Claudio, and Lila, had disappeared. I read about Azucena Villaflor de Vicente. Her son Néstor, and his fiancée, Raquel Mangin, had been abducted. Azucena searched for Néstor and Raquel and met other women looking for missing children. On April 30, 1977, after six months of enquiries that came to nothing, Azucena led a small group of women to the Plaza de Mayo in Buenos Aires, where they walked in front of the Casa Rosada, the government house. Gatherings of more than two people were forbidden, so the women walked in pairs, arms linked. On December 10 that year, Azucena was taken by force from her house and never seen again.

For half an hour every Thursday afternoon, the mothers and grandmothers still walked in a circle around the Plaza de Mayo, carrying photos of their lost loved ones, wearing white kerchiefs embroidered with names and dates of disappearance. The kerchiefs, originally diapers, represented their children.

From 1976, the year I was born, to 1983, children were kidnapped or stolen from women who had given birth in prison after months of torture. In "death flights," people were drugged and thrown from cargo planes or military helicopters into the Atlantic Ocean or the Río de la Plata. New terrors crept into my dreams.

In the record collection that belonged to the older sister of my friend Julie, I found the U2 album, *The Joshua Tree*. The title of the last song jumped out from the album cover. "Mothers of the Disappeared." On Sting's *Nothing Like the Sun*, I found "They Dance

Alone." I used all my allowance to buy those records and played them so many times I almost wore them out.

My mother finally broke the silence. One evening, when I had the newspaper spread out on my bed and was listening to Sting for about the thousandth time, I didn't realize she was there until she sat on the edge of the bed.

"Don't worry, *mi amor,* I know you're not reading the comics." She lifted the needle on the record player on my bedside table. "Papá and I think it's time we talked to you about your grandmother." She put her fingers under my chin, made me look straight at her, and took a deep breath.

"You know that many people, thousands of people, disappeared in Argentina – sons, daughters, parents, grandchildren, grandparents, uncles, cousins, aunts, brothers, sisters, and friends. They were taken by the government police from their homes, from the streets, from parks, from schools. Your *abuelita* was one of those people who disappeared. I am so sorry that we didn't tell you this before, but we didn't know the right way or when to say it. We didn't want to frighten you, and I guess we were just hoping that we would find her.

"Even before the worst times, it started to be very dangerous for us. At the university, we had to be careful of everything we did or said. Anyone suspected of disagreeing with the government could be arrested. We were very scared. Professors were being fired and some students disappeared. That's why we had to leave, before it happened to us. Your father was right. He saw it coming. His parents and sister had already left Argentina and were living in France. He was invited to give a talk at the university here in Peterborough, and when we saw what was happening in Argentina, we decided not to go back." My mother took another deep breath and stopped talking for what felt like ages. I was afraid to move, sure she was going to start crying, but this time, she didn't.

"My mother – your *abuelita* – was last seen walking along Matheu Street one morning. She waved goodbye to her neighbour, Señora Luz, and said that she was going shopping. She didn't come home that day. She never came home."

As I listened, my head was spinning. The room was spinning. Husbands like my grandfather would return home to half-prepared meals, a knife on the counter beside a plate of potatoes, a bag of onions, a shopping list, a neighbour's story of some men in sunglasses in a Ford Falcon with tinted windows and no licence plates.

"Why did they take her, Mami? Why? What did she do?"

"She was an innocent, Ale. She didn't do anything wrong. I think the police were looking for me because of some articles I wrote, criticizing the government. Your *abuelita* and I have the same name – Marcela. We heard the stories about people disappearing, but we never thought that it would happen to us.

"We were so far away and Lito was alone, but he refused to come to Canada even when we begged him. It took two years after your *abuelita* disappeared for us to convince him. He was so sure that he would find her again. He still is. He wouldn't leave because he thought that she might come home one day. He refused to stop imagining she would, even though so many people didn't come back. He tried everything, searched everywhere that he could think of, filled out many, many documents, but she had just vanished.

"Before Lito left Buenos Aires, he visited Señora Luz. He gave her our address and telephone number in Canada and made her promise to contact us when your *abuelita* came home. He told her that he was going to be back in Buenos Aires soon. He was just going to visit his family in Canada for a while to see his new granddaughter. I think you are the reason he stays here with us, Ale. He has someone who listens to his stories. I never did. Now, I sometimes wish that I had." She rubbed her fingers against her forehead. "With you, he can at least feel a little happy again. But it's very hard for him here. Buenos Aires will always be his home."

"Why can't we find her, Mami? Why? Is she dead?"

"I don't know, *mi amor,* but we're still looking for

her. I promise we'll never stop. I'm going to Argentina to do a test – a blood test to try to help find your *abuelita*. It's called a DNA test. She and I have the same DNA in our blood, just as yours is like mine. They will try to match it with the DNA of people who disappeared."

"You mean the dead bodies of people who disappeared, don't you?" I slammed my fists into the bed, wouldn't look at her. "Please don't go to Argentina, Mami. What if they kill you?"

"Nobody is going to kill me, *mi amor*." She gently rubbed my shoulder and kissed me on the forehead. "We have to do something and we don't know what else to do. Papá will be there with me. We'll stay in Lito's apartment. It will only be for a couple of weeks, and Lito will take care of you while we're away."

"When did she disappear?" My voice was shaking as I struggled to get the words out past the lump in my throat.

"It was in 1976, Ale, about two months after you were born."

My mother put her arms around me and buried her face in my hair. Only when I realized she was crying could I let my own tears come. I hugged her as tight as I could, afraid for her, wanting to comfort her, protect her, as she'd tried to protect me.

I didn't need to hide my notebook in my schoolbag anymore.

My parents left for Buenos Aires at the end of June. While they were away, Lito and I made our meals together. He would put on his tango records and sing along while showing me how to roll out the dough for empanadas and make pasta from scratch.

"Your *abuelita* is a much better cook than me. Her food is delicious."

He sometimes talked about her in the present, as if she might walk through the door at any moment. I knew it wasn't just because of mistakes in English. I guess he sometimes just needed to feel she was alive and needed me to believe it with him, even just for a little while. I suppose I needed to believe it too. He knew my mother had told me about what had happened to my grandmother. I knew he knew that I knew, but we didn't talk about it.

For the first few weeks after my parents came back from Buenos Aires, all I could think about was the letter that would arrive from Argentina with news that they'd found my grandmother. I would race home from school every day with the same question. And every day, my mother's answer was the same. "No, Ale, nothing yet. It might take a long time before we hear anything."

Eventually, I stopped waiting for that letter. Sometimes there is no magic strong enough to undisappear someone, no matter how hard you believe.

∞

I moved to Toronto for university and lived in a small apartment on the third floor of a house on Brunswick Avenue. In Peterborough, the only time I heard Spanish was in Lito's stories and tangos and in conversations between him and my parents. My parents always spoke English with me. Even Lito did a lot of the time. In Toronto, it was easy to find Spanish – in the stores along Bloor and College, in the student lounges at the university, or on the streetcar along College or Bathurst.

When my parents and Lito came to Toronto to visit me for the day, we would walk down to Kensington Market and buy empanadas at the Chilean bakery on Augusta Street. Lito made friends with everyone, joking and laughing with the woman behind the counter, the cooks in the kitchen, and the other customers. He would put his arm around me and tell them all that his *nieta* was so smart and she was in university. Often, he would repeat the stories, forgetting he'd already told them, but no one seemed to mind. I'd never seen him like this. He was different in Toronto, recharged by the bustle of the city. Even though he'd begun to forget all kinds of things and couldn't walk very fast anymore, he always dressed up for our outings in a sparkling white shirt he'd ironed himself the night before. I would tell him he looked so handsome and I really meant it. In the coffee shop up the street from the bakery, he would order for the four of us, introducing us to the Colombian waiter again each time we were there.

When the weather was warm, we would drive to Harbourfront. I always expected to hear more stories about the deep, dark Río de la Plata, but Lito was more interested in stopping at one of the carts along the lake that sold sausage on a bun, which we'd eat while sitting on one of the benches and watching the boats.

"Not as good as the *choripan* you can buy from the carts on the Riachuelo, but not bad," he pronounced. "Too bad that they don't have *chimichurri* instead of that sweet stuff. What do you call it? Rayleesh? Next time, I will bring some *chimichurri* with me!"

On the way back, we would stop off at Honest Ed's department store on Bloor Street, where he dragged us from floor to floor, buying things he thought we needed – sandals for me, a scarf for my mother, slippers for my father. Later in the afternoon, we would take a thermos and a blanket and walk slowly to the park near my apartment, where we sat under the trees, sharing *mate*. After so many years, I felt we were all freer. We laughed more easily. I wished we'd come to Toronto sooner, when Lito and I could have taken the streetcar together along College Street. And for a while, I was free of the nightmares.

On nights I couldn't sleep, I would call Lito and ask him to sing me a tango, but the silences on the line gradually became longer and more frequent. When this happened, my mother eventually took the phone and was the one who sent me a goodnight kiss. After that first year in Toronto, my parents began to visit me on their own. Each time I went back to our house in Peterborough, it got harder and harder to bring Lito back to me.

I made copies of his tango records and took the tapes with me to Toronto. Some nights, I would dance alone in my apartment, my eyes closed, my whole body infused with D'Arienzo's driving two-four beat. I would fall asleep to Caló's "Pedacito de Cielo"* or Canaro's "Poema."

I met Cameron in the lounge of the International Student Centre at the University of Toronto during my second year. I felt him watching me, and when I finally looked up from reading *Cien Años de Soledad,* I guess I gave him enough of a smile to encourage him to start a conversation.

"Good book?"

"Yeah."

"I see you're reading in Spanish. I have to work on mine. Always good to read in the original. What's the title in English?"

---

* Little Piece of Heaven

"*One Hundred Years of Solitude*. It's by Gabriel García Márquez."

"Oh, yeah, right. I have a copy. Mine's in English, though. Been meaning to read it, but I've got a pile of other ones I have to get through for my courses first. I'm doing my Master's in Political Science."

I wasn't sure what to say next. The rest of our first conversation consisted mostly of a lot of talking from him and lots of nodding and the occasional "yeah" from me. I don't think he really wanted much more than that. He seemed to be pretty happy just hearing himself talk.

After a few weeks of our hanging out with his friends, who threw around words such as 'praxis,' 'socio-economic analysis,' and 'epistemological shift' and knew Che Guevara's last words to the soldier who shot him, and attending talks by his professors and other graduate students, Cameron started introducing me as his girlfriend. Actually, I got the uncomfortable feeling that he only saw me as a possible source for his research because my parents came from Argentina. His specialty was Latin American politics and he already fancied himself an expert. His knapsack was stuffed with pages and pages of notes and photocopies. The shelves in his room were packed with books on Latin America. The first thing you saw when you walked in was a life-size Che Guevara poster. He was a wealth of information and it didn't take much to launch him into a lecture. I think he believed he could single-handedly liberate the oppressed of the world. He insisted on constantly wearing a poncho he'd bought somewhere on Bloor Street, saying, any chance he got, that it had been made by Peruvian villagers.

He was also trying to learn Spanish and I sometimes felt like a dictionary. His pronunciation was laughable, but it felt mean to tell him that, so I didn't. He was trying after all. But I really hated it when he called me Alexandra or, worse, Ali. There were lots of other things I didn't tell him, and I was afraid to take him home to meet my family. My father taught Political Science, and I could just imagine the silence at the dinner table and the look on Lito's face when Cameron started spouting off.

I think I was using him as much as he was using me. He knew all about *Las Madres* and oppression, not just in Argentina. But he hadn't listened to the Sting or U2 songs and had absolutely no interest in tango. He certainly couldn't dance and resisted any attempts I made to show him even one tango move. We had long conversations that usually ended in fights, in which I'd insist that popular music and culture, Argentine tango, for instance, could teach us a lot about history, and he'd say he was happy to leave that stuff to the cultural anthropologists. I didn't tell him that was my mother's job. One day, all the stupid details add up to a pile you can't just ignore or work around anymore. When I realized I wanted to protect La Renga, El Ciego, El Dentista, La Bonita, and the others from people like him, I knew we would end, probably soon and probably badly. And my nightmares came back.

When I turned on the television late one Friday night for a break from studying for my exams, I finally watched *The Official Story*, the film that had won the Oscar when I was a kid. The woman in the film slowly discovers that her adopted daughter may be the child of a *desaparecida*, a woman who disappeared during the last military dictatorship in Argentina. She finds out that her husband has known about this all along. When she finally confronts him, he tells her to stop asking questions. She decides to leave him and takes her daughter to her mother's house. When her husband demands to know where their daughter is, she asks him how it feels not to know where his child is.

In the final scene, the daughter sings a song that was very familiar to me – the children's song "En el País de Nomeacuerdo"* by the Argentinian writer María Elena Walsh. When I was little, Lito used to sing María Elena's songs to help me fall asleep. And some mornings, we would dance around the living room to "Manuelita la Tortuga," about a turtle who tries to change her life by going to Paris, and "El Reino del

---

* In the Land of I Don't Remember

Revés,"* about a land where everything is upside down and backwards.

I studied astrophysics at university. Maybe it was because of all Lito's stories about El Loco and the stars. Among the few things Lito had brought from Argentina was a physics book. He told me El Loco had given it to him. It was full of mathematical equations, and there were formulae and notes in a language I didn't recognize scribbled in the margins. Turned out it was Czech.

From 1911 to 1912, Einstein was a professor at Prague University. I found a picture of a plaque that stands outside a house in Prague's old town square, saying that Albert Einstein played violin and met his friends, the writers Max Brod and Franz Kafka, there in the salon of Mrs. Berta Fanta.

Before Einstein, Newton's Law of Universal Gravity had dominated physics. In Einstein's four-dimensional space-time continuum, light didn't travel in a straight line but bent near objects with gravitational fields, such as our sun, and the curve due to gravity would be twice that predicted by Newton. We only see the stars at night. During the day, the sun is too bright to measure how much the light from stars bends near it, except during an eclipse of the sun.

On the morning of May 26, 1919, two scientists,

---

* The Kingdom of Reverse

Andrew Crommelin and C.R. Davidson from the Royal Observatory in Greenwich, sat on the racetrack of the Jockey Club in Sobral, Brazil, waiting for the eclipse. Luckily, no races had been scheduled for that day. When the sun crossed the bright Hyades star cluster, the starlight passing through the sun's gravitational field would be visible. Measuring the daytime shift of the stars from their position at night would determine whether Einstein or Newton was right.

May is the rainy season in Sobral and the sky was overcast, so the scientists were afraid they wouldn't be able to photograph the eclipse. Luckily, just before the six minutes of total eclipse, the sky cleared. Their pictures confirmed Einstein's predictions and made him famous.

Reading about Crommelin and Davidson on the racetrack in Brazil made me think of El Dentista waiting at the racetrack in Buenos Aires for a glimpse of Claudia. I scratched for connections. In the university library, I pored over photos of Czech physicists and the scientists waiting for the eclipse that would test Einstein's theory. I was searching for a thin young man in a black hat. There really was a snowstorm on June 22, 1918 in Buenos Aires. Could El Loco have met Einstein in Prague and been off to Brazil during that snowstorm to watch the eclipse the following year? I drew pictures of El Loco in the margins of my textbooks, and while I should have been studying for my exams, I often found myself looking for articles on Argentina.

I learned that Alfredo Ignacio Astiz, a twenty-two-year-old Argentinian naval lieutenant and intelligence officer, had infiltrated the Mothers of the Plaza de Mayo by posing as Gustavo Niño, telling them his brother had disappeared. On December 8, 1977, as the group was leaving a meeting at the Santa Cruz church in the San Cristóbal neighbourhood of Buenos Aires, Astiz' embraces signalled to soldiers watching from a distance who in the group should be arrested.

Azucena Villaflor, the founder of *Las Madres*, sat beside me in the library, looking over my shoulder as I read about Einstein, eclipses, and Astiz. She stared back at me when I looked in the mirror. In some of my dreams, she walked with my grandmother. In others, I lay in a cold concrete cell in the basement of the Navy School of Mechanics in Buenos Aires, listening to the cries from others being tortured, knowing that no one would ever find me, my belly expanding with hunger, fear, and the child growing inside me. Or I was naked, groggy, shivering in a helicopter above the Río de la Plata. But Lito was not there to soothe me back to sleep. His memories were disappearing, but the more he slipped away, the stronger the presence of the people in his stories became.

A black hole is formed when a huge star is dying and implodes. It is silent, invisible. Its gravitational force is so strong that nothing can escape from it, not even light. Einstein's theory of relativity predicted that at its centre is a singularity, a one-dimensional point with infinite density and gravity, where laws of physics can no longer be applied. The fabric of space-time ruptures. It's the point where everything we've previously understood means nothing and predictions are impossible.

When I finally told Cameron his Spanish was awful and it was about time he washed his goddamn stinking poncho, he stormed out of my apartment and I didn't hear from him for three weeks. One afternoon, he called and asked me to meet him for drinks at the Imperial Pub on Dundas Street "to clear the air between us."

When I got there, it was obvious he'd already had a few drinks. He had his arm around the woman beside him. So much for clearing the air.

"Hi, Ali. Good to see you! Glad you could join us. Have a seat. I've already bought you a beer. This is Paola from my Spanish conversation group. And this is Silvio. He's from Argentina. We've just met him. He was sitting alone at the next table, so I invited him to join us." Cameron punched Silvio in the arm and grinned. Silvio nodded at me and raised his glass.

"Paola's parents are from Peru," Cameron announced as I sat down. He was trying hard to impress her, and me, rambling on one minute about his poncho and the next about a book he'd started reading – *Theologies and Liberation in Peru.* As usual, when he'd had a few drinks, he just couldn't shut up. He wasn't making much sense.

"You are quite an expert on Latin America, Cameron." Silvio said. "Have you travelled there?"

"Yes, Mexico, with my parents. When I was fifteen, we had a week in Cancún. It was a real eye-opener."

"Yes, I can imagine."

If Lito had been there, that was exactly what he would have said.

"So many poor people working for peanuts." Cameron shook his head slowly. "That's when I knew I had to do something."

"Something?"

"Yeah. Then, in first year, I read Freire's *Pedagogy of the Oppressed* and it totally influenced me. Education is the way out of oppression. That's why I decided to major in Poli Sci."

"Paulo Freire, the Brazilian writer?"

"Yeah, that's right."

"I will be interested to hear your ideas sometime, Cameron."

"Sure, yeah, sure, sometime. Not now, though. I promised Paola I'd walk her home in a few minutes."

When Cameron finally stumbled out the door with Paola, I felt nothing but relief to be rid of him, his poncho, his political analysis, and his whispering and giggling in Paola's ear. I still had half my drink left and was trying to decide whether to leave or stay. I gave Silvio an uncomfortable smile. He smiled back and winked at me from across the table.

"Your friend is quite an idealist."

"That's one way of putting it. He can also be a pompous ass when he gets going. You're *porteño*, right?" The only way I could tell Silvio was surprised was that his eyebrows went up. "I recognize the accent. My parents are from Buenos Aires and my grandfather likes to call me a *porteña*."

"I bet your *abuelito* has a lot of stories."

"Yes, lots of them. I like to listen to him. His memory's going now, and I've started to write them down so they're not forgotten."

"And I imagine that he dances tango in the kitchen." My turn to look surprised. Silvio smiled. "All the old guys in Buenos Aires do that. The floor is nice and smooth, they are close to the *mate*, and it doesn't cost anything to dance in the kitchen. My *abuelo* was the same. He had a tango for every situation. My father does too. Cheers to the old guys and their music." He raised his glass and finished off his drink. "Well, I think I'm ready to go. Your Peru expert left and I don't think he's coming back. This is not Buenos Aires, so no *milonga* for you to go to, but how about a *cafecito*? But I warn you, I can't dance. Maybe you can tell me one of your *abuelo*'s stories."

And, for the first time in my life, as we walked along the street, that was exactly what I was doing.

The next morning, I took the streetcar down to the lake. It was snowing lightly and the icy wind off the water cut through my jacket as I walked along Queen's Quay towards Harbourfront Centre, where Silvio had told me he shared a workshop.

It wasn't hard to find him. I could feel the heat from the kilns as soon as I turned down the corridor that led to the studios. He had his back to me and was focused on a man wearing a plastic mask and thick gloves, who was putting an amber-and-green glass vase into a kiln. Silvio's light-blue T-shirt, streaked with sweat, clung to his back and hung loosely over his thin frame.

I watched him for a few minutes, not sure what to say, waiting for the right moment to speak. He closed the kiln door and nodded when he turned and saw me.

"Hi, Silvio. I thought I'd come and check out what you do."

"Hey, Ale! Happy to see you. This is Carlos." Carlos flipped up his mask, smiled, and gave me a quick wave. "We just finished that piece we put into the kiln. It has to cool down in there for a few hours. I'm going next door to Queen's Quay Terminal to get something to eat. Wanna join me?"

"Sure."

"OK, if you can wait a little while I clean up, we can go together. You can tell me some more stories."

"Yeah, OK. I've never seen anyone work with glass before. It's fun to watch." Fun. Not exactly the word I was looking for. I felt awkward, unsure, struggling for words. If he'd noticed how nervous I was, it wasn't obvious.

"It's a delicate balance," he said as he hung up his goggles and gloves and checked some gauges. "You heat something hard and brittle until it's flexible enough to shape. And then you roll it on the marver – that steel table over there – to make the form that you want. Then you breathe into it to expand it, but through a tube from a distance, or you get burned. After that, you roll and shape it with your hands, using a cloth soaked in water, and then your co-worker breathes into it, expanding it even more. You have to trust each other. You need a lot of patience. Each step must be repeated many, many times until you get exactly the form you want. Heat, cool, shape, heat, cool, shape. Over and over again. It feels like meditation sometimes. You don't think of anything else.

"All the elements are there – fire, air, water, earth. Glass is silica, basically sand. I like doing this because you are making something beautiful, fragile, and full of colour, easily broken at each stage of the process. If it cracks, it's useless."

"I would cry if something broke after all that work."

He looked at me over his shoulder and smiled. "You are too sensible, girl. If it breaks, you just start again and make another one." The Spanish *'sensible'* translates to 'sensitive' in English. Lito always mixed these words up too. I thought of what El Loco had said to Tito when Manuel ripped up his words. "Instead of trying to put the old words back together, you could write new ones. That way you'll never have to be afraid of anyone destroying what you've written because you know you can write more."

We walked across the parking lot to Queen's Quay Terminal.

"When I breathe into the tube, I imagine that I'm filling the glass with what is in my head – songs and even poetry. Words and music between the molecules. Something like that anyway. I know it probably sounds strange." Silvio shrugged and smiled.

When he talked to me, he made me want to know everything about him.

Silvio lived in a house on Pembroke Street. I got off the subway at Dundas and had to weave through an assortment of swaying hookers and off-kilter drunks while dodging puddles of melted snow. A man standing in a bus shelter gave me a wink and the once-over as I passed. His stomach bulging out under the bottom of his jacket and his greasy hair made me think of Armando Rodríguez.

Huddled on the front steps of the house where Silvio lived were two guys wearing frayed sweat pants and ski jackets and a woman in a bright-red sweater and pink jeans. They each had a cigarette in one hand and a can of beer in the other.

"Hi. I'm looking for Silvio."

The woman ran a hand through her straggly blond hair and smiled. "Oh yeah, you want the Spanish guy with all the pieces of coloured glass. I think he's in. Second floor at the back." She nodded towards the front door, which was half open. They moved aside to let me pass.

I went up the stairs and knocked on a door at the end of a dingy hallway that smelled like cigarette butts and old carpet. Silvio opened it into a room filled with afternoon sunlight and shelves lined with multicoloured glass bottles and jars. Flashes of cobalt, vermillion, ultramarine, viridian.

"Come in, Ale." He smiled and kissed me on the cheek. He took my coat and hung it on a hook on the inside of the door, on top of his. Pieces of glass hung from fishing line in the windows, scattering rainbows that danced on the walls, the ceiling, and the single bed. In the corner was a small table covered with sketches. A shelf above the table held a couple of mugs, a bag of coffee, a few plates, and a coffee press.

"Welcome to my home. Not a palace and I have to share the washroom, but the neighbours are OK and the rent is cheap. The landlady, Margaret, is nice. She lets me pay every week."

"I like it. Lots of light."

He smiled. "Yes, and it's much better than the hostel where I lived my first days in Canada. I had only eighty dollars in my pocket when I landed in Toronto. It was February. My first job was to shovel snow. I waited on the corner in the mornings for the truck to pick me up and they paid me at the end of the day. Never been so cold in my life! My boots leaked when they got wet, so I put plastic bags inside them. After a few days of work, I left the hostel and found this place.

"The truck driver was from Uruguay. He introduced me to his friend Carlos, the guy that you met in the workshop last week, and Carlos invited me to work with him. He's from Argentina too, from Mendoza, and he helped me a lot. I took some glassblowing classes in Buenos Aires, so I had a little experience, and he liked some of my ideas. We make stuff to sell in the gift shop beside the studio. My life is much better now. Much warmer too."

He saw me staring at a small photo that was propped against a blue-and-white glass bottle on a shelf in the window. A young couple are dressed for a summer evening out, he in a white shirt and tan pants and she in a blue dress and red high heels. They're dancing in a close embrace. One of her feet is delicately poised, ready to take the next step.

"Those are my parents when they first met," he said quietly. "They are still crazy about tango, especially my father, just like his father was. See that box over there? It's full of cassette tapes. My father sends them to me. He records tangos from the radio and adds his own commentary. The tapes are always wrapped in letters full of details like what he and my mother had for dinner and breakfast and lunch, fixing their car, and what they are going to do tomorrow. They are still in love after more than thirty years. Every morning, they get up very early, share *mate*, and talk. When I ask them how they stayed together so long, my mother always says that those morning conversations never got boring." He smiled. "Anyway, sit down at the table and I will make us some coffee."

He cleared the sketches off the table and moved them to the bed and then plugged in the kettle. "My father made me study English. He said that maybe it will be useful for me in the future. He was right, as usual. Sometimes he even asked me to translate tango lyrics for him. But the words don't sound the same in English. He shrugged. "Some things you just can't translate."

"And you don't dance tango?"

"No way! It was what my parents did. My friends

and I liked rock and roll more."

"Too bad. I could teach you some."

"Remember, I have two left feet, as you guys say in English."

"I don't believe you! If you listened to tango music all those years, you must have learned something."

"OK, you win. Let's try. The coffee can wait. Just please take off that disappointed face." He kissed me on the forehead.

"Embrace me." I looked straight at him and put my hands on his shoulders.

He wrapped his arms around me and we didn't move for a long time. I repeated what Lito always said. "Just close your eyes and listen to the music. Your feet will move by themselves." I hummed the first few bars of "A Media Luz."*

Slowly, silently, we began to dance.

∞

Silvio's arms are traced with lines of thin white scars. One night, while we're lying in bed, I ask him how I got them.

"I was an active kid. Lots of cuts and bruises. I fell out of a few trees and off a few roofs."

"I don't believe you."

"You don't have to." He turns away from me and

---

* At Half-Light

stares at the ceiling, one arm under his head. I feel the way I used to when I was afraid to ask my mother questions, so I shut up.

"And you, Ale? Why did you study physics? What makes you so interested in Einstein?"

Instead of talking about the paper I'm writing on Einstein's 1925 visit to Argentina, I tell him about El Loco's hat and how he taught Tito to read. About the stars that look different in the Plaza Dorrego and the snowstorm in Buenos Aires. I guess I think he might get it.

Maybe I need to tell someone else in case something happens to me and there's no one to remember the people in Lito's stories.

One afternoon, as I go up the stairs to his room, the door is open and I hear him whistling.

"What tango is that?" I ask as I enter. "I don't recognize it."

"It's called "Qué Noche!" What a night! My father told me that Agustín Bardi wrote the music on the night of that famous snowstorm in Buenos Aires."

I know Lito's people are safe.

Lito used to say that two people should dance tango as one body with four legs. Silvio says he doesn't dance, but there's music in every one of his movements. Measured, present, he knows exactly the right moment to pause. Whatever he does, it's the same, whether he's making coffee, telling me a story, or working with Carlos in the studio. They can go for hours without talking, every movement coordinated, focused.

In our kitchen, he does what we call his morning dance, which I never get tired of watching – taking the coffee down from the shelf, spooning it into the espresso maker with one hand, the other hand turning on the stove, tapping out a beat with a spoon on the table.

A pause. And then he turns to face me. "OK. I got them after I went to jail. It was a game."

"Got what?"

"These." He points to his arms. "The scars. Remember you asked me about them?"

I didn't expect this. I haven't mentioned the scars for months. He sits across from me at the table. I'm afraid to move in case he stops talking.

"I have one for every time that I was picked up by the police. You did it yourself to show how tough you were, how much pain you could take. Sometimes it was a way to stop getting beaten up. It also made you forget the fear for a little while."

"Some game!"

"Yes, and that is enough about it. You don't need any more pictures in your dreams. It's too crowded in there already."

"What?"

"You talk in your sleep, Ale. *Abuelita, desaparecida, Azucena.*"

"Stop protecting me. My parents used to do that. If I only half-know things, I start imagining and my dreams just get worse."

"Maybe I'm protecting myself. I need to concentrate on now, forget the past a little, or at least remember slowly." His voice is very soft.

I think of my parents – my father, who always had his nose in a book, and the missing ends of conversations when I walked into the kitchen. I always thought they'd just been protecting me, but now I think that perhaps they also needed to remember slowly, focus on now, and create a new present for all of us. Otherwise, my mother might have been crying all the time. They always spoke English with me. Even Lito did a lot of the time. The fabric of tango is made from what has been lost – a patchwork of nostalgia, pain, and longing – but it's danced in the present. For a few brief moments, all that matters is connection with your partner, with the music, with now.

But the ghosts of the past have a way of invading the present, finding ways through cracks in the silence, sliding in through the half-light.

"How long were you in jail?" I know I'm pushing it and get ready to change the subject. I'm good at this. I've had lots of practice.

But he doesn't turn away. "Which time? Mostly

overnight stays. I was lucky. When the really crazy times started, I was only a kid, so I managed to stay out of trouble, but when I got older, it was more difficult. The police didn't need a reason to arrest you. No one carried an address book because they might look through it and take names. For some reason, they always let me go."

He leans on the counter and stares past me. "My mother always gave me shit for staying out all night, but I couldn't tell her what happened. I knew that if I said anything, she would probably go to the police station and demand to know why I was arrested. That would only make trouble for all of us, so it was a bad idea to tell her, or anyone. You were afraid to talk to anyone. That's how that kind of system works. Fear of everyone and everything. You did not want to call attention to yourself in those days."

I sit very still and wait for him to continue.

"Some people were not so lucky. One of my friends, Santiago, and his older brother, Tomás, were picked up by the police one afternoon. They let Santiago go, but we never saw Tomás again. He was only sixteen, Ale. When Santiago came home, he shut himself in his bedroom for days and wouldn't talk to anyone.

"Anyway, want some coffee? It's ready." He opens the cupboard and takes out two cups, spinning them around on his index fingers by the handles.

"Yeah, sure. Thanks." I know there's no point

asking more questions, but I also know that, just like La Bonita, I've wedged my foot in the door before it completely closed.

I'm alone in a dark house with brick walls a foot thick. There are narrow stairways leading in all directions. Up, down, up again. Some of them lead nowhere except to heavy wooden doors that are locked or slam shut when I reach them. Some lead me back to where I started. My heart is pounding. I'm trying to catch my breath. From the top of one stairway, I can hear Lito calling me. His voice is very far away and getting fainter. Frantic, I run up the stairs towards his voice, but when I get to the top, I find another door. I turn the handle, but it's locked. I slam my shoulder into the door, kick at it, but it won't budge. I panic, spin in circles with no idea which way to go. I run back down and try another stairway, but this one leads up to a ledge overhanging a precipice.

"Wake up, Ale. It's OK."

When I open my eyes, I'm not sure where l am. All I can see is Silvio's face. The rest of the room is out of focus. All I can feel is his hands on my shoulders.

"Tell me one of your stories," he says.

Silvio doesn't talk in his sleep. He's silent, his body still. When we were first together, I would sometimes watch him as he slept and wonder what he dreamed about or if he even dreamed at all.

Some nights, I wake up and he isn't beside me. I get up and find him sitting at the kitchen table drawing or looking out the living room window into the darkness. Some mornings, he gets up very early and goes to his workshop and is back before I wake up. When he gets into bed, I can feel the warmth of the kiln as he breathes words and music into me. I fold myself into him, my fingers tracing the curve of his shoulders, the small of his back, the few strands of grey that run through his hair, the thin white scars along his arms, the parts of his life I don't know, might never know. The memories that have made me afraid are second-hand, passed on from others, but, filtered through my imagination, they've claimed me anyway, can paralyze me. Silvio's silence is different from mine, and the things that crawl into my sleep and wake me are having to make room for him.

Sometimes the door opens without my having to push, and other times, it swings wide open.

The World Cup, July 4, 1998 in France. Claudio López has just scored for Argentina in the quarter-finals against the Netherlands. At eighteen minutes into the game, the score is 1-1. The bar is packed. Lots of blue-and-white football jerseys. Silvio is about the only one not chanting "Ar Gen Tiiii Naaaa!"

"OK, enough football. Let's go out for a walk." He

downs the last of his drink.

"Come on, Silvio. It's tied. Argentina might win."

"You can stay and watch it if you like, but it's pretty noisy in here, and I know a very nice, quiet place we can go where they have good coffee and cake." He winks.

Coffee. The solution for everything. He grabs my hand and we wind our way through the mob out onto College Street. We pass a Portuguese bakery full of soccer fans yelling at a small TV screen. I'm a bit dizzy from drinking so early in the day and the quick exit from the bar. The bright sunshine is making me squint. We walk a few blocks in silence.

"I really don't feel like coffee or cake, and if you're not going to talk to me, Silvio, I don't feel like walking anywhere with you!"

"OK, let's talk about football."

"I thought you'd had enough football for today."

He turns to me as we wait for the light at Bathurst Street. The look on his face is hard to describe – a mix of sadness and confusion and something else I have no name for. But I know it well. It's the expression he gets when he talks about his friends Tomás and Santiago.

And then the door swings open.

"I remember during the 1986 World Cup, I asked my father why he wasn't interested in watching it," he says. "Like most of the guys in Argentina, I was crazy about football. At first, he didn't want to talk about it, but he eventually told me about the 1978 final. I was just a kid when Argentina won the Cup for the first time, 3-1 against the Netherlands.

"My father's face was very serious and he told me to just sit down and listen. He said we should never forget that the River Plate stadium, called the Monumental Stadium during that 1978 World Cup, was not very far from ESMA, the Navy School of Mechanics, where people were being tortured and five thousand prisoners were held, sometimes six of them in a cell of less than three square metres – about five by six feet. They had to eat rotten food and many were sick or dying. *Las Madres* were demonstrating because the international journalists were there. It was a chance to show everyone what was happening in Argentina. The world knew that people were disappearing and what the dictatorship was doing, but the world was doing nothing.

"They say that the sound from the crowd when Argentina won its first World Cup was like a jet engine taking off, and the prisoners for sure heard people in the street cheering and celebrating. Years later, we learned that if the prisoners didn't cheer hard enough or look happy, the guards beat them. Some of them were even dragged out of their cells and driven, only half-conscious, around the city to watch the celebrations. For some people in Argentina, every four years, the World Cup brings back all those bad memories, opening the wounds again."

At Augusta Street, which leads to Kensington Market, a car is turning right. As the driver stops to let us cross, I am awash in images of Lito entertaining the people in the empanada shop and the cafés. And then dark ones. Another car in another city – a Ford Falcon slowing down and dragging us inside, taking us to a room where unimaginable things will happen to us. On another street on a sunny morning like this one, my grandmother had disappeared.

I want to run, but I take Silvio's hand and hold on tight, forcing my feet to fall in step with his. We walk in silence across Spadina, past Chinatown and the university. We sit on a bench in Queen's Park and watch three boys kicking a soccer ball around.

"The president of Argentina, General Jorge Rafael Videla, was never at a football game before, but he went to seven games of that World Cup," Silvio says. "He invited Henry Kissinger, the American Secretary of State, and his family. Big party. Big distraction from all the country's financial problems and the people who were disappearing. Kind of like what Mussolini did in the 1934 World Cup and Hitler did in 1936 in the Berlin Olympics.

"The government did everything that they could to make Buenos Aires look good. They bulldozed some of the *villas*, the slums, just knocked them down and moved thousands of poor people who lived there out of Buenos Aires.

"General Videla visited the locker room of the Peru team before the semi-final, and some people believe that the game that got Argentina into the finals was fixed – that Peru agreed to lose the game in exchange for Argentina accepting and holding political prisoners from Peru. The Condor Plan – cooperation between dictators in Argentina, Brazil, Chile, Bolivia, Paraguay, Uruguay, Peru, Ecuador, and El Salvador. Ramón Quiroga, the goal keeper for Peru, was originally from Argentina. The rest of the world helped – America and who knows which other countries. Everyone was afraid of communism, so they supported the dictators. I wonder how the American people would feel if they knew that their taxes paid for training and equipment for torture."

One of the boys kicks the soccer ball hard and it lands a few feet from where we're sitting.

"Good shot, kid!" Silvio stands up, waves at the boy, and kicks the ball back. "Feels very good to kick something. OK, let's walk some more and find a café. The game must be over by now."

We head back along College Street and pass a group of guys talking in Spanish about the game. "2-1 for the Netherlands. Shit! I can't believe Bergkamp scored at ninety fucking minutes!"

When we get to the Free Times Café, the TV is off. No football fans in sight. We sit at a table at the window, order coffee and cake, and stare out the window until it arrives.

"Three World Cups later, in 1990," Silvio says, "I watched the people in Buenos Aires celebrating, shouting, and cheering for Argentina's team, and all I could think about was those prisoners in 1978, sick, shoved together in filthy cells stinking of urine and shit and eating rotten food, their wounds infected, their blood on the walls of the torture rooms, with no one to hear their screams except their torturers and the other prisoners. I wondered if that was where they took Tomás."

His right hand contracts into a fist that he slams into his left palm. He looks right at me. His voice is almost a whisper. "Can you imagine thinking that no one knows where you are, and if you die, your family will not even have a body to bury?"

He picks up his cup and takes a couple of slow, deliberate sips. He stares down at his plate and moves pieces of cake around with his fork.

"Later in 1990, we got the news that President Carlos Menem was giving pardons to General Videla and some other military officers. Videla was only in prison for five years of the life sentence that he got in 1983 for murder, kidnapping, torture, and many other crimes. I remember Menem on television, saying something about starting to build the country in peace, liberty, and justice again. Most people knew that it was bullshit, only a way to get the military on his side so that he could stay in power. And Videla even had the nerve to demand that the military get an apology. An apology, Ale!

"There were big demonstrations against the pardons. Forty thousand people marched from the Plaza de Mayo to the Congress, shouting and carrying banners with the names and photographs of people killed or still missing.

"I remember it was a Sunday, the day before New Year's Eve. That day, I sat in a café near the Congress and thought of Tomás, wondering what happened to him. I always will."

"Tell me more about Tomás, Silvio. What was he like?"

He sips his coffee and doesn't say anything for a while. He takes a deep breath.

"OK. He was tall, much taller than me. And skinny. Blue eyes, hair always a mess. Sometimes we skipped school and sneaked into football games. He was good with his little brother. Both of their parents had to work a lot because they didn't have much money, so he took care of Santiago.

"Tomás had an old guitar that his father gave him and he carried it around everywhere. He was a good singer, loved rock and roll. He told Santiago and me that he was going to join a band and travel all around the world and play music and we could go with him.

We had plans to get on a boat and sail to Europe, find jobs, and meet lots of pretty girls. I think of him a lot, and sometimes I see him broken and bloody and can almost hear him screaming. I hope, if he's dead, he died quickly."

He stares into his cup and runs one hand through his hair. I've never seen him this close to tears and I'm not sure what to say, so I just reach across the table and touch his cheek. He takes my hand and gently kisses my fingers.

"His mother kept his guitar. She believed that she would find him one day. When she could get time off work, she used to go to the Plaza de Mayo on Thursdays to walk with *Las Madres*. Santiago was never the same after his brother disappeared. He was always angry at everything and everyone, even me. Didn't want to talk to me anymore. He was drinking too much, doing a lot of drugs, and couldn't keep a job. One day, he was hit by a truck, or maybe he walked straight into it, and one of his legs and his nose were broken. His face is full of scars and he limps. My father told me that he still lives with his parents. I write to him, but he doesn't answer my letters.

"I sometimes imagine walking down a street somewhere in the world and Tomás walks up to me with his goofy smile and scruffy hair and hugs me, slaps me on the back, and gives me his usual '*Che, boludo.*' And then we go to find Santiago. That's how I keep

Tomás out of my dreams – imagining him alive, breathing him into pieces of coloured glass.

"Thousands of people – people like your parents and Lito and Santiago and his family – live with the horrors of that time and the ghosts of people who will never come home. For them, the dead will never rest. That's why *Las Madres* continue walking in the Plaza de Mayo, and maybe it's why Lito told you those stories about your *abuelita*. To keep her alive, to keep believing that she will come home one day. Living without hope is a terrible thing."

I think of my mother, sitting on my bed, finally telling me about what had happened to my *abuelita*. I eventually stopped waiting for that letter from Argentina, but I know she never has.

"I was lucky, Ale. I *am* alive. That Sunday morning in the café near the Congress, I made the decision to leave Argentina. Maybe it was partly for Tomás. He never had the chance, but I could do it for him. My parents gave me the money for my ticket to Toronto."

At home that evening, we fall into bed, exhausted. We wrap around one another, very still. I feel the rise and fall of his chest, each breath he takes. My fingers on his shoulder, his arm across my chest, my thigh against his, a strand of his hair on my forehead.

"By the way," he whispers, "In 1988, your friend Sting and a bunch of famous musicians – Peter

Gabriel, Bruce Springsteen, Tracy Chapman, and some others – gave a concert in the River Plate stadium. Sting invited *Las Madres* to the stage and they came on in a line, holding hands. They had pictures of their lost relatives pinned on their chests. Some of them were very old. Sting sang "They Dance Alone" in Spanish. Peter Gabriel joined him, and the two of them danced with *Las Madres* right up there on the stage. Seventy thousand people were there, all of us shouting and demanding justice, including me. I will never forget it. We owe a lot to *Las Madres*. They will never let us forget."

He kisses my forehead and slides out from under the covers. He goes to the window and opens the curtains. "*Media luna.* Half-moon tonight."

I go to him and rest my body against his back, my arms around his chest.

"Listen. How peaceful the streets are," he says. "No cars."

No Ford Falcons without license plates driven by men in sunglasses.

"Come back to bed, *mi amor.*"

We make love slowly, carefully. One body with four legs.

Just as I'm drifting into sleep, he says, "And I've just remembered something that you can see in photos of that 1978 World Cup game. A guy named Carlos Loiseau, Caloi, used to draw a comic in the *Clarín* newspaper of a bird with no wings called Clemente. Clemente encouraged people to throw pieces of paper onto the field at the games, a 'paper rain' campaign, even though the government was trying to stop this football tradition during the World Cup. They wanted everything on the field to look clean. The military thought Clemente was just a cartoon and didn't pay attention to his sarcastic comments about how the government was using the World Cup to paint a good picture of Argentina and hide what was really happening. The FIFA technicians, not the generals, controlled the big screens on the football field. At the final game, Clemente suddenly appeared on the screen and said, 'Throw the confetti, boys!' The field was covered with small pieces of white paper. In the pictures, it looks like snow."

It's still dark when Silvio kisses me goodbye the next morning, and I go back to sleep. Later, when I get up, I find a sketch on the kitchen table of a striped, wingless bird in the middle of a snowstorm. It's wearing a black hat covered in stars.

∞

On a bright morning in August, we go down to the terminal on Bay Street and catch a bus to Peterborough. It's Silvio's first time out of the city since he arrived in Toronto. The bus goes east along Dundas on the way to the highway.

At Pembroke Street, he points north. "My old room is up there. I wonder how Margaret, my landlady, is. And those guys who were always on the step drinking beer and smoking. It's only been a few months, but all of that feels so long ago."

He pronounces the names of the streets, marvelling at the English spelling. Berkeley, Parliament, and Sackville become *Berk e lay. Par lee a ment, Sack vee jay.* "Ah, River! Finally one that I can say." Up the Don Valley Parkway along the river past the Brickworks to the 401. When we pass Ajax, I know what's coming. *"Ah hax."*

"Stop it, Silvio! Just enjoy the ride. You sound like Lito every single time he passed the sign for Peterborough. *Pe tair borro ug ha.* That used to drive me crazy. He would laugh his head off."

As we pull into the bus station in Peterborough. I can see my mother and father waving. This is their first time meeting Silvio. He jumps off the bus first and takes my hand as I get off. He doesn't let go of it as we walk towards my parents, who have big smiles on their faces. I hug both of them at once.

"Mami, Papá, this is Silvio."

*"Es un gran placer conocerlos a los dos. Finalmente!"** Silvio kisses my mother on the cheek and gives my father a

---

* It's a great pleasure to meet you both. Finally!

hug. As we walk to the car, the three of them are talking easily in Spanish, like old friends who haven't seen each other for a long time and have a lot of catching up to do. *Porteños*. My mother tells Silvio to call them Marcela and Julián.

We're greeted at the door of our house by the young woman who comes in to look after Lito when my parents aren't home.

"Carla, this is Alejandra and her friend Silvio," my mother says.

Carla smiles and welcomes each of us with a smile and a kiss on the cheek. "It's great to meet you, Alejandra. Your parents have told me all about you. Marcela, your papá is sleeping in his room right now. I made some sandwiches for his lunch, but he wasn't hungry, so I left them in the fridge. Maybe he'll eat them later. OK, I'm sorry I have to run. I have to pick up my son from school."

"Thanks, Carlita. Say hi to Matthew. See you the day after tomorrow."

My father takes Silvio on a tour of the house and then they go down to the river. As they head out the door, I hear them talking about their boat trips along the river to Tigre.

My mother puts on the kettle and we sit at the kitchen table. "We're lucky to have Carla," she says. "Her parents are from Chile and she speaks some Spanish. When Lito speaks, it's only in Spanish now.

We just don't like leaving him alone. When we put on his tango music, he sometimes sings along. It's the only thing he seems to recognize."

Suddenly, Lito is standing in the doorway. His clothes are rumpled from being slept in. He still has a full head of hair, but it's almost white now. He's wearing slippers we bought on one of our trips to Honest Ed's years ago.

"*Mate?*" he says.

"*Sí papá, el agua está casi lista. Vení aca y sentate con nosotros. Mira! Ale está.*"*

"Lito!" I jump up and give him a big hug. He looks at me, expressionless. I search his face. Nothing. No flicker of recognition. I lead him to the table. My mother prepares the *mate* and passes it to him. We sit in silence for a while. My mother gets up and slips a tape into the deck. Alberto Castillo with Tanturi's orchestra.

Since Lito has chased English out of our house, I switch to Spanish too. "*Bailamos*, Lito?" I take him by the hands and stand him up. "Just listen to the music and your feet will move by themselves."

He just stands there, so I pull my mother up and lead her around the kitchen. She steps on my foot a couple of times.

"Ouch! Mami, you're a really lousy follower! Where

---

* Yes, Dad, the water is almost ready. Come and sit with us. Look! Ale is here.

did you learn to tango?"

"I did not. Obviously."

"Just close your eyes and listen to the music. And stop thinking!"

"Impossible!"

"Come on. Just try!"

Halfway through the song, we're both laughing so hard we're crying. Lito turns to watch us, the almost-imperceptible beginnings of a smile on his face. When he sings the first line to "Así se Baila el Tango," we both throw our arms around him.

The first thing Silvio and my father see when they come back in is the three of us in one embrace, dancing to Alberto Castillo. Tango holds our memories so we can dance in the present.

After lunch, Silvio and I walk down to the river with Lito. Silvio takes his arm and I carry the cassette player, *mate,* and thermos. Silvio and Lito sit in two of the three Muskoka chairs and I lie on the ground, eyes closed, the sun on my face, and listen to the river called Otonabee, "the river that beats like a heart."

If you are very still, you might hear secrets whispered by the rivers.

"*Che, gitana rusa,** do you want to have some *mate* with us?" Silvio says.

And then Lito sings, his voice strong, the first line to "Gitana Rusa." Silvio sings the next line, and the

---

* Russian gypsy

three of us finish the tango together.

For dinner, we eat a full-on Argentinian meal at the picnic table in the garden. My mother has made *empanadas de carne* and *chimichurri,* and my father opens a bottle of red wine that one of his colleagues brought back from a recent trip to Mendoza. He and Silvio put steaks on the barbecue and carry on a running conversation about the types of beef – *bife de chorizo, vacio, lomo, bife ancho, tira de asado* – and how they should be cooked.

"Slowly."

"Yes, for sure, very slowly."

"Over hardwood coals."

"And you should only use salt. None of that terrible barbecue sauce!"

"And you need to eat it with really good, fresh bread."

"And *chimichurri,* of course*"*

My father slaps Silvio on the back. "The next time you come, Silvio, we'll build a real *parilla* and I can throw out this stupid little barbecue. Lito's been bugging me to do that for years."

I've never seen my father slap anyone on the back before or heard him call our barbecue stupid. I've never heard him talk this much. Perhaps it's the wine and the freedom of speaking in his own language. He talks and talks and talks.

"The story of Argentina – one government out, another government in, some much worse than the one before. The seventies were not the first time we *argentinos* suffered. One coup after another. Always repression, murders, corruption. Argentina owed money to the whole world. It used to be a rich country. And then fifty-percent inflation in 1951, the peso down seventy percent! My father worked like a dog all his life, but his money was worth less and less. In 1983, ten thousand old pesos were only worth one new peso. And it kept getting worse. Public services were a mess. But you know all this already, Silvio."

Silvio nods. "Yes, one of our neighbours had to wait ten years just to get a telephone line."

"That *cabrón*, General Galtieri, even started a war with England in the Malvinas to distract everyone from what was happening. We have a history filled with pain. Lots of material for tango. People who are looking for hope put their fear, disappointment, sadness, and despair into music, and they dance. That's all they can do." My father slams his fist on the table. "I love my country. I miss so much about life there, but tell me, how can anyone live in such a place?"

They talk about people who are lost. Silvio tells them about Tomás and Santiago. When my mother talks about my grandmother, my father puts his arm around her shoulder. Every so often, he brings her hand to his lips and kisses it. My mother's stories about my *abuelita* are different from Lito's. Some are a child's stories of birthday parties and surprises and going to the market on Saturdays to buy things for cooking special Sunday treats.

I look at Lito and wonder how much of this he's taking in. He hasn't moved or said a word all evening. I move closer to him and rest my head on his shoulder. By the time we finish eating, it's dark. I wonder if he can see the river shimmering with stars.

That night, Silvio and I sleep in the double bed in my old room, where I had once pored over the *Toronto Star* and the dictionary, trying to break through the silence; where my mother had finally told me about what had happened to my grandmother; where, so many times, Lito had gently put me back into bed after turning my nightmares into dreams of rivers full of stars and a beautiful woman with soft dark hair.

"Thank you for today," Silvio whispers as we slide into sleep.

∞

"I want you to listen to something." Silvio pushes the play button on the cassette deck. A woman sings a tango in a voice that sounds as if it's filtered through gravel. Defiant, impossible to ignore.

"Who is she?"

"Tita Merello, one of the few famous women tango

singers. She's one of my father's favourites. He sent me this tape a couple of weeks ago. She was a very big star in the movies and on TV. I think she might be the one who was in room number 15 – La Niña Bonita."

"What? Why do you think that?"

"So many details that Lito told you fit her story. Her real name was Laura. Her father died when she was a baby and her mother couldn't afford to take care of her, so she lived in an orphanage until they thought she had tuberculosis and sent her to the country to work on a ranch. She started singing in theatres and clubs in Buenos Aires when she was about twelve, I think. She was tough, had a difficult life. But Lito already told you all that, even if he invented or changed the details about some of his old friends a little. He was only a kid when he heard some of those stories.

"I was thinking about those numbers of the rooms in Lito's house too. They sound like slang for numbers for the *quiniela,* the lottery in Buenos Aires. 15 is *la niña bonita.* 22 is *el loco.* 37 is *el dentista.* The story of El Dentista and his bicycle made me laugh. *Bicicleta* means a shady financial deal in *lunfardo*, originally the slang of criminals in Buenos Aires – a language they used to hide secrets from the police. Many people choose their lottery numbers by what appears in their dreams. If you dream about water, you choose the number 1, *el agua.* If you dream about a bird, 35, *el pajarito.* People really believe in this stuff. Once, a woman even went to the police to accuse another woman of entering her dreams to steal her numbers. Imagine that!" He shakes his head and smiles.

"Tell me about Tita Merello."

"OK, but take some deep breaths first so that you don't pass out." He kisses me on the forehead.

"She went into exile in Mexico after the military *junta* in 1955. They persecuted anyone who did well during the previous government, when Perón was president. She even worked in an amusement park for a while because she couldn't find any other work in Argentina until that government was kicked out in 1958.

"Tita is in her nineties now and she's not well. Maybe you should go soon. My father says you can find her in the Favaloro Foundation on Belgrano in Buenos Aires."

Silvio puts his arms around me and, as I listen to La Bonita sing "Se Dice de Mí,"[*] I'm not sure if the tears on my face are mine or his and who is protecting who.

"I can't go with you. Not yet," he says.

"It's OK. I know."

∞

On the morning of my flight to Buenos Aires, Silvio is gone before I wake up. On the kitchen table, I find a

---

[*] They Say about Me.

tiny blue glass bottle sitting on a note.

I breathed some of Expósito's words about not forgetting into this one. See you when you come back. I will be here. I hope you find them all.

Un refuerte abrazo.[*]

S.

RETURN

Yo adivino el parpadeo
De las luces que a lo lejos,
Van marcando mi retorno.[*]

On February 12, 2001, I leave twenty-seven centimetres of snow in Toronto and, the next day, step off the plane into a summer afternoon in Buenos Aires. María Elena's song, "El Reino del Revés," which Lito and I used to sing, is running through my head. Here, the seasons are reversed, the constellations are upside down, and the sun moves across the sky from right to left.

Other passengers are being greeted with *porteño* nicknames. *Che, boludo! Como estás, gordito? Que pasa, colorada? Tanto tiempo, flaca!* From all directions, I hear words I learned from Lito. He compressed Buenos

---

[*] I imagine the flickering / Of the lights that in the distance, / Will be marking my return. (From the tango "Volver." 1934. Music: Carlos Gardel. Lyrics: Alfredo Le Pera.)

Aires for me and, now that I'm here, his world is bigger than I imagined. I want to see his face, have him here with me. I need him to take me to the *patio de tango* and walk through the big house with me so he can show me where El Ciego's room is. I want to sit with him under El Loco's tree in the patio where Gloria danced with the *malevos* and La Bonita sang his tangos.

In the taxi from the airport, I'm finding my words, my thoughts, in Spanish, laughing with the driver, telling him about Lito and how we dance in the kitchen in Canada. And he's complaining about Argentina – the traffic, the price of food, inflation, and the unexpected strikes.

"Every Friday, there's something new. Sometimes you take a plane somewhere and can't get back because the airline is on strike. And next, it's the newspaper kiosks. So many people with no money, no jobs. There will be riots again soon. If I were smart, I'd get out, but this is my country," the driver says, shaking his head, the way you complain about a relative you love but drives you crazy, someone you want to leave but can never abandon.

"*Bueno,* señora, since your grandfather was from Buenos Aires, you are *porteña.* Tango is in your blood." He turns up the radio. "Listen to that! 'Yo Soy de Parque Patricios.' The two angels – Ángel Vargas singing with Ángel D'Agostino's orchestra. From the forties. What a voice!" He sings along, very loud.

"Aaah, Parque Patricios! That's the *barrio* I'm from."

Matheu Street, the last place my grandmother was seen, is in Parque Patricios.

I settle back in the seat, happy to listen, not wanting this ride to end. I drink in the streets. Everywhere looks like downtown. Profiles of couples at tables in cafés. Animated conversations on street corners. I'd be happy to drive around all day like this. Too soon, we arrive at Balcarce Street.

"OK, we're here." The driver points to a house on the right. When I pay him the fare, twenty American dollars, he hands it back and wags his finger at me. "I know all the *yanqui* money looks the same, but this is one hundred dollars." I exchange the hundred-dollar bill for a twenty, feeling thankful and a little stupid. He gives me his card. "Call me if you need a taxi. My name is Ángel, like D'Agostino and Vargas." He grins. "I have a safe taxi, always safe, but *ojo*, be careful with the others, *linda.*"*

I'm shown to my room on the second floor by Gabriela, who runs this house for tango tourists with her mother, Ana, who is away in Mar del Plata.

"My mother and her friends are probably drinking sangría on the beach right now. They do this holiday once a year. They're all psychologists. They say that half the people in Buenos Aires are psychologists and the other half are seeing one." Gabriela laughs. She

---

* pretty girl

slips easily between English and Spanish.

I unpack my bag, put my clothes away, and lie down but can't sleep. I sit on the single bed, not sure what to do next, so I get up and go into the kitchen, where I find Gabriela drinking coffee.

"Not tired?"

"I tried to sleep, but it didn't work, so I gave up."

"Well, there is an afternoon *milonga* on Bartolomé Mitre this afternoon if you want to go. It starts at three and goes until ten." Gabriela looks down at my feet. "Do you have anything besides those running shoes?"

We go back to my room and, after I show her the shoes I've brought with me, she frowns, not impressed. "OK, no problem. We're about the same size. I can lend you some. We can start with some heels that are not too high."

At El Arranque, my first *milonga*, Gabriela instructs me on how to behave. "We have to change our shoes in the washroom before we go into the *salón*. Never do it inside. It's bad manners."

We change our shoes and go in. Gabriela is greeted with a kiss on the cheek by the man at the door and he leads us to a table.

"This is my mother's usual seat," Gabriela says quietly. "Everyone can see you here, and it's easy to know if you're being invited to dance."

At four in the afternoon, there are at least three

hundred people there. Lots of grey-haired or balding men in suits and older women, some with their hair bleached bright-blonde, who are effortlessly balancing on three-inch heels. Men and women are seated on opposite sides of the room at rows of tables covered with checkered cloths. There are also separate areas for couples and mixed groups. The dance floor is polished stone.

Gabriela whispers more instructions. "Make sure you look friendly and happy. No one wants to dance with a person with a sour face. It is very important to follow the *códigos,* the rules of the *milonga.* Wait for a man to make eye contact. If he keeps looking at you, and only if you want to dance with him, smile and nod, but wait for him to walk over to your table before you stand up. Keep looking at him, but let him come to you. If you accept an invitation, you must dance with him until you hear the *cortina* music after three or four tangos. It's not tango music and gives everyone a chance to change partners."

Sure enough, after one tango into the next set, the DJ plays Fresedo's "Tigre Viejo,"* and a guy who looks to be in his seventies is nodding at me from across the dance floor. I smile and nod back as instructed. I used to play this game of *cabeceo* with Lito, but this time, I'm not in our kitchen or down by the lake, and he's not here. The man walks towards our table, and when he's

---

* Old Tiger

a couple of feet away, Gabriela discretely nudges me to stand up.

We wait for a break in the line of dance and then merge onto the dance floor. He's a little shorter than me. He embraces me firmly but gently, and we're off. I remember Lito's advice and try not to think, to just listen to the music and follow. I'm surprised how comfortable it feels to dance with this person I've just met.

When the music stops after our first tango, he says, "I no see you before. Where you are from?" It looks as though word has already gone around the room that I'm not from Buenos Aires.

"Canada. Toronto."

"But your tango it is very good. Where you learn?"

Listening to him struggle in English is painful, so I switch to Spanish and see him relax. "My grandfather taught me. He's from Buenos Aires."

"Ah, that's why!"

After two more tangos, when the DJ plays some Donna Summer, he escorts me back to my seat, smiling at Gabriela.

"Well, I can see that you'll be OK on your own at a *milonga*," she whispers. "Just ask for my mother's table and you'll get a good seat. They all know her. Otherwise, if they don't know you, you'll probably get stuck at the back and won't get many invitations to dance."

"Who is he, that guy I was dancing with?"

"His name is Rodolfo. He's a good dancer. He's here every week, and you will also see him at some of the other *milongas*. My mother told me that his wife died a couple of years ago and he lost his only son – one of the disappeared – during the 1980s. I was very young when all that bad stuff happened, but we're learning about it now. I think tango is the only thing that keeps Rodolfo going." She shakes her head slowly. "And that's how it is for so many of these guys. You will see them at the other *milongas*, always sitting in their regular seats. The *milonga* is a place where, just for a few minutes, the tango you're dancing to is the only thing that matters. Tango is like breathing for them. And it's the one thing that they're sure they will never lose."

As we're walking towards a taxi stand after the *milonga* that night, Gabriela asks me why I've come to Buenos Aires. I'm not sure what to say, where to start. There's a storm raging inside my head.

"A bunch of reasons. Kind of hard to explain. My grandfather was an orphan and grew up in a *conventillo* here. I wanted to see all those places he told me about when I was little. He can't come back, so I thought I would. He's losing his memory. I guess I came as a kind of promise to him not to forget. Also, my grandmother disappeared here. In 1976."

Gabriela gasps.

"My mother's mother. We still don't know what happened to her. Her name was Marcela – the same name as my mother."

Gabriela stops walking and, when she turns to look at me, I can see the tears in her eyes. She suddenly throws her arms around me.

"Oh, Ale, I'm so sorry! I didn't know."

"It's hard to explain, but I need to be in places she was once, walk on the same streets."

"Yes," she says, wiping her eyes with her sleeve. We continue walking.

After a few minutes of silence, Gabriela says, "There are so many terrible stories here. I have a friend who discovered that her parents are not really her parents. I can't tell you her name because I promised not to tell anyone. A few months ago, some women came to the office where she works and told her that her real parents had disappeared and were killed. They found her mother's remains, but they can't find her father's. A military couple took her when she was a baby and changed her birth certificate, gave her a new name. At first, she didn't believe it, but she had a blood test and it was true. She says she sometimes wishes she didn't know, that they never told her, and she didn't take that blood test."

"My God! What do you think she'll do?"

"I don't know. She cries a lot now and has bad dreams. She's angry and doesn't know what to do. She says she still loves the people she thought were her parents, but now she hates them too for what happened. Imagine discovering at twenty-two that your family, the people you loved, lied to you your whole life! Imagine if they told you that the person you thought was your father could be responsible for killing your real parents. They say that maybe five hundred babies were stolen. Sometimes when I'm on the bus or the subway or sitting in a café, I look at the faces of the people around me and try to imagine which of them would be capable of doing those horrible things."

In the taxi on the way back, we don't talk, just stare out the windows.

"Go to see *Las Madres* in the Plaza de Mayo on Thursday," she says as she hugs me goodnight. "I sometimes go and walk with them. Some people here want to forget the bad things, the suffering, but I believe that we need to remember or it could happen again. The government needs to know we will not forget. The world needs to know."

∞

I stand outside Retiro Station as the clock in the Tower of the English strikes three and think of La Bonita – Laura – a child of only about twelve, arriving alone in Buenos Aires with only a bit of stale bread and a tattered map, looking for her mother.

Gabriela has warned me to watch my bag and try not to look like a tourist when I'm near the station.

"Lots of pickpockets there. On one side of the railway tracks are the big apartments of Recoleta, but on the other side, behind the station, is Villa 31, an area where a lot of really poor people live. Yes, there are still *conventillos* in Buenos Aires. People also take the train in from outside the city to see what they can steal. Like going to work every day to make money."

Sitting on the ground, huddled together against the station wall, are a woman in a long flowered skirt and two children. The boy, just a few months old, is crying. The girl, about four, is making flowers from scraps of coloured tissue paper and wire. The woman holds out her hand. Her slender fingers are streaked with grime.

"*Por favor, señora. Para mis niños. No tenemos nada pa' comer.*"*

I give her a few pesos, which she stuffs into a pocket in the folds of her skirt. The little girl smiles and offers me the pink flower she's just made. I drop it into my bag, smile back, and wait a few seconds, half-expecting her mother to whisper a secret, but she just nods and looks away, focusing on a woman behind me.

I follow La Bonita's route from the station. Along Libertador past Plaza San Martín, down Reconquista, across Corrientes to the Plaza de Mayo, and I see them – *Las Madres*. The mothers and grandmothers of those who disappeared during the military dictatorship are slowly, methodically, circling counter-clockwise, as

---

* Please, señora. For my children. We don't have anything to eat.

they've done every Thursday afternoon for almost twenty-five years. Walking in circles, the way they did in government and police offices and prisons, looking for answers, only to be told to return another day. Their white kerchiefs are embroidered with *Aparición con Vida*[*] or the names of their lost children and the dates they disappeared. Photos of the missing are pinned to their chests. Decades of heartbreak and resolve are etched on their faces.

I'm not sure what I thought I would find here, but I didn't expect this silence. Perhaps that's what grief and hope turn into after so many years of sadness, anger, and loss.

I fall in behind one of them and surrender my silence to theirs. I think of Azucena, her son Néstor and his fiancée, Raquel. Renée Epelbaum's children – Luis, Claudio, and Lila. Silvio's friend Tomás. My grandmother Marcela. I put one foot in front of the other and, with each step I take, I repeat all the names I remember.

Two women in white kerchiefs sit at a small table covered in leaflets and books. *Cantos de Vida, Amor, y Libertad.*[†] *Círculo de Amor Sobre la Muerte*[‡] *by* Matilde Mellibovsky. *El Mundo Guarda Silencio*[§] by Laura

---

[*] appearance alive
[†] Songs of Life, Love, and Freedom
[‡] Circle of Love over Death
[§] The World Stays Silent

Bonaparte. I flip through *Escritos de Jóvenes Secuestrados.*[*]
It's a book of poetry by students, each poem preceded
by a page stating the name of the writer, a birthdate,
the date of disappearance, and a picture from a
government-issued identity card. *El Corazón en la
Escritura*[†] is for sale.

As I'm paying for the book, my words spill out. "*Mi
abuela.* Her name is Marcela Torres. She disappeared.
In 1976. They're still looking for her. My mother gave
her DNA."

"*Ay, mi amor.*" One of the women stands up, takes
my face between her hands, and looks straight into my
eyes. Her face is lined with years of sorrow and
determination. She kisses me on the cheek. When she
hugs me, I feel the strength in the hands pressing into
my back. She strokes my hair the way Lito used to and,
just for a moment, I feel I'm being held by the
grandmother I've never met. The sky is split by a flock
of birds taking off. My insides crack open.

As I'm leaving the Plaza de Mayo, I see a man about
Silvio's age taking the arm of an older woman who had
been walking with *Las Madres.* She is tiny, so thin. The
man drops his cigarette and stamps it out before giving
her a kiss on the cheek. He has a limp. He's wearing a
pair of baggy jeans that look as though they haven't
been washed for a while and a faded green T-shirt with

---

[*] Writings of Kidnapped Youth
[†] The Heart in Writing

a small rip in one shoulder. His hair is tied back in a ponytail, and his face has the beginnings of a beard that partly hide the ragged scars on his face. I immediately think of Santiago and Tomás and their mother, who Silvio said sometimes walks with *Las Madres* on Thursdays. I run to catch up with them.

"Santiago? Excuse me, señor, are you Santiago?"

They turn around. The woman is about to say something, but the man silences her with a look.

"I am Silvio's friend." I search his face for traces of recognition – a raised eyebrow, a twitch at the corner of his mouth. But nothing.

"Silvio?"

"Yes. He's in Canada now. In Toronto."

"No, sorry. You've confused me with someone else, señora." He shakes his head and takes the woman's arm and they walk away, arms linked. I half-expect them to turn around and walk back. I watch them until they're lost in the crowd.

I walk along the Avenida de Mayo past the Café Tortoni. Fragments of memories come at me from all directions. I promise myself I'll come back later for a *chocolate*. It takes me three light changes to get across Nueve de Julio, the widest street in the world. I can see Lito's Obelisk up the street at Corrientes. I stop for a few minutes outside the Teatro Avenida, where, according to Lito, more than eighty years ago, La Bonita got kicked out of the first show she auditioned for, *The Virgins of Teres*. The theatre door is locked, so I can't go in.

I turn at San José and walk down to Hipólito Yrigoyen. At the Café de las Madres, I order coffee and sit down. One wall is covered with photos of people who disappeared. I feel hundreds of pairs of eyes staring down at me, burning into me – women and men of all ages, some no more than teenagers.

An old man with a straggly white beard is sitting at a corner table under the photos, watching me. He could be Lito's age. I smile and he nods. At a *milonga*, this would be the signal to dance. I have a million questions but can't find the words or the nerve to get up and walk the twenty feet to his table. He stirs his coffee and I stir mine. I try to imagine the things he's seen, what he's lost.

I leave the café and walk back to San Telmo. At Balcarce and Chile, where El Delicado – the guy in Lito's tango – had stood eyeing the girls, a very old man stands beside a small table outside a café, smoking, with a small glass of amber-coloured spirits at arm's length. His frayed three-piece suit was elegant once. He sips from the glass and then places it carefully on the table beside his silver cigarette case. I do a quick calculation. El Delicado would be at least a hundred now.

I go into the fruit and vegetable store on the corner. The man at the counter is probably in his fifties. Too young, but I decide to ask anyway.

"*Hola,* señor. I'm looking for La Renga's house."

"La Renga?"

"Yes. Doña Pepa. Josefa. The Rodríguez family used to live there. And Manuel and Tito."

He shakes his head. I buy two apples and continue retracing La Bonita's steps. The lottery shops are everywhere. Some of them are only a few feet wide, just openings in the wall with a banner saying *Quiniela.* I buy a couple of tickets, using some of Lito's numbers, the ones for the people in my dreams – 15, *la niña bonita*; 22, *el loco;* 37, *el dentista*; 55, *los gallegos.* For La Renga, 77, *las piernas*, the legs. And 48, for the dead who speak.

On Sunday, I go to the fair in San Telmo. Tables are piled high with memorabilia – antique soda syphons and phonographs, bracelets fashioned from coins made worthless through endless rounds of inflation, tango and movie posters, rusty street signs, sheet music. Tools, used clothing and books, lines of *mates*, incense. A magician is pushing cigarettes though cards and making a piece of red silk appear and disappear. His fingers move quickly, but I can spot some of the old tricks Lito taught me. There's a crowd around an old couple who are dancing cheek to cheek to music by a tango duo on guitar and *bandoneón.* The man is wearing a dusty pinstriped suit, a grey fedora, and the typical white *milonguero* scarf. The woman is in a tight bright-red skirt and black fishnet stockings.

I walk back along Defensa, imagining Armando's drunken walk with El Dentista, looking for the house with the tango patio. On the opposite side of the road, a skinny woman who looks at least seventy, wearing a black miniskirt, fedora, gloves, fishnets, and sparkly silver heels, is swaying to tango music coming from a small boom box on the ground beside her. Her hair is frizzy and bleached. Propped against the wall behind her is a piece of cardboard on which she's pasted a Carlos Gardel poster, a few photos of herself dancing, and a handwritten sign that says *La Maleva de San Telmo*, the bad woman of San Telmo. When a couple of tourists try to take her picture, she scowls, shakes her fist, and points to the pink plastic bowl at her feet.

I stop outside a big house that's now a gallery of shops and feel this might be the place I'm looking for. The heavy front door could be the one where La Niña Bonita begged La Renga for a room and Armando, propped up by El Dentista, yelled to be let in. The door is wide open. I go in, holding my breath. In the central courtyard – the patio – I see what must be El Loco's tree and where Gloria waited for Señor Rodríguez and danced with El Puño's *malevos*.

La Renga's room at the front is closed, a cat stretched out on the doorsill. Looking for Tito's loose tile, I find one that's cracked, the broken pieces glued back in not quite straight. I scuff at it with the toe of my running shoe.

Outside Dolores' room stands a vacant-eyed mannequin in an orange tango dress. To its left is a pile of twisted metal, splintered wood, and shards of leather and canvas, which take shape in places to form parts of iron beds, backs and seats of chairs, table tops, a steamer trunk, a cracked, twisted dog collar, and a rusted bicycle, the front wheel mangled, the spokes broken. I pull images from the pile, extracting memories. I toy with the idea of pulling the bike down and wheeling it around the patio. I reach up to ring the bell, but it's too rusted to work.

El Dentista's room at the back of the patio is now a small shop. On a shelf outside it, among used running shoes and slippers, is a pair of shoes with heels higher than I've ever dreamed of wearing – ebony-and-emerald marvels. I go in and ask the woman sitting in the corner if I can try them on.

"Excellent choice!" She takes the shoes from the shelf and sits me down on a small stool. After doing up the buckles on the ankle straps, she holds both of my hands and helps me to my feet. I take my first few uncertain steps forward.

"They are perfect for you, señora, and almost new," she says. "Now, you will dance even better!"

I hand her the fifteen pesos. She wraps the shoes in brown paper and drops them into a plastic bag. They are now my responsibility.

The stone steps to the second floor are worn smooth and bowed after a century and a half of footsteps. I hold onto the railing and close my eyes, feeling my way up the stairs, towards the sky, my fingers searching for El Ciego's, and I count the steps the way he did. *Un.* I feel Armando on the bottom step, watching Tito sing to La Bonita. *Dos, tres.* La Renga pausing on the stairs before patrolling the patio. *Cuatro, cinco.* Gloria's midnight walks. *Seis, siete, ocho.* There is a dark stain on the eighth step. Blood? But I can't feel La Chica here. Perhaps her footsteps were too light to leave an impression.

Stopping outside El Ciego's room as I move along the corridor on the second floor, I can imagine La Rusa's children crying, a woman cursing, Armando shouting, and the thud of flesh against stone. Tango slides through the crackle of static on a radio – Pugliese's "Gallo Ciego."[*] El Loco's room is now a small café. At one of the three tables in the corridor outside it, a man and woman are drinking coffee.

Downstairs under El Loco's tree, I reach into my bag and run my fingers over Doña Pepa's piece of glass to find the familiar rough edge. As a child, Lito imagined it was a piece of his mother's star. He gave it to me one summer night when we were sitting beside the river in Peterborough, looking up at the sky. The

---

[*] Blind Rooster

doors of this house will be closed before it's dark enough to see the stars from the patio, so I go out to the Plaza Dorrego.

After walking around the bench in the plaza, I reverse direction and walk around it again. I sit down and inch along it, moving from one spot to another, trying to feel where Tito and El Loco used to sit.

I hear Carlos Gardel singing lines that slide through me. I follow the music to the bar across from the plaza. The typical black-and-white tiled floor. Photos of Borges, Gardel, and other icons on the walls. An ancient gold espresso machine, now unused, sits above windowed drawers that are hand-labelled with the names of supplies sold here when this was also a general store – *polenta, queso, yerba, maíz, arvejas, azafrán, galletas, pimiento.* The small wooden tables and bar are covered with graffiti, much of it impossible to read. More than a hundred and twenty years of names carved over other names – lovers, friends, and favourite football teams, each with a story. I choose a table beside the window and order a *café con leche* and three *medialunas* from the formally-dressed waiter. I imagine El Dentista peering nervously through the window at Armando, who is slumped over the table across from me after one too many glasses of grappa.

That evening, as it gets dark, sound equipment is set up for a *milonga* in the plaza. A couple who look to be in their eighties arrive, their arms linked. Everyone seems to know them and hugs and kisses are exchanged. I can't help but imagine Lito and my *abuelita* at that age. The music begins – a tango I've heard so many times before. Alberto Castillo sings "Así se Baila el Tango." That's how you dance tango. They start slowly, settling into an embrace. For them, at this moment, time stands still. There is only now, only this soft summer night in Buenos Aires. After years of moving to the same music, they dance as one. One body with four legs.

As a child, I used to imagine the night sky as El Loco's hat, and in some of my dreams, the stars were tattooed on the inside of my skull. El Loco said the stars are different above the bench in the Plaza Dorrego. I hold Doña Pepa's piece of star up to the sky and it catches moonlight, starlight, the street light.

Lito never told me which star was his, but I know it's Sirius, the brightest one, which I can also see in Toronto. I want to tell him that Sirius is actually a binary – two stars that orbit one another, bound together by forces that come from their centres.

∞

The woman at reception in the Favaloro Foundation says Señora Merello is not accepting visitors at the moment.

"Are you a relative?"

"Well, no, but my grandfather used to know her."
She doesn't believe me. I can feel it. She's probably
turned away hundreds of people with stories like mine.

"I'm sorry."

"But I've come all the way from Canada to see her."

"I'm sorry. It's not possible."

I go back the next day and three days after that. I
try going at different times, hoping I'll get a different
receptionist, but every day, it's the same one. Every
day, the same answer. I'm about ready to try to sneak
in somehow, but I have no idea where La Bonita is, and
this hospital is a big place. But on my fifth unsuccessful
try, as I'm walking towards the exit, a young woman
comes up behind me, taps me on the shoulder, and says
quietly, "Come with me. I know you've been here every
day for almost a week."

I follow her along a corridor, up a flight of stairs,
and down more corridors until she stops and points to
a half-closed door. "I can't promise she'll see you, but
we can try." She motions to me to be quiet and goes
into the room.

After a few minutes, she comes out, shaking her
head. "I'm very sorry, but she says no."

I am so close. "Please! Please tell her I'm Tito's
granddaughter. Tito, Alberto Torres. She sang his
tangos. They used to live in the big house in San Telmo
with La Renga, El Ciego, El Loco, El Dentista, and
Gloria. On Defensa." I suddenly realize I'm shouting.

213

And then, all of a sudden, the door slowly opens and there she is – a tiny, ancient woman, her grey hair tied back in a ponytail, her perfectly-manicured hands holding onto the door frame for support. She's wearing a white cardigan with black polka dots, a black skirt and shoes, and a purple-and-green scarf, as if she's ready to go out somewhere special.

"Well, *chica*, I'm not sure I remember your grandfather, but even if none of what you're saying is true, you certainly have a good imagination. La Renga, El Ciego, El Loco, El Dentista, and Gloria. Oof! That really sounds like a tango, *piba*! I haven't heard a good new tango in years. I suppose we'll have to let this one in, Nina."

Nina smiles and kisses her on the cheek. "Yes. Please go in. I'll be right outside. And take your time," she whispers.

Tita arranges the pillows on her bed and settles back. "OK, *piba*, I am listening. Let's hear your stories. But only for a little while because I get tired easily these days."

I sit in the chair beside the bed and tell her about El Dentista's bicycle, El Ciego and La Chica, La Renga's sweeping and cursing, Tito's tangos, La Rusa's babies, El Loco's hat full of stars, Gloria, and the *malevos*. She just listens and I catch her humming. I think it's a tango, but I'm not sure.

After a while, she closes her eyes, but I keep talking,

talking, talking, and when I can't talk anymore, I sing the first line of Lito's tango. "*Flaco, fino, y delicado.*"

"*Durito muy bien parado,*" she murmurs. "You know, *piba*, I was only about thirteen when I sang in the cafés on the Avenida de Mayo. Only twelve when I was in the Bataclán. It was a rough business. Nobody thought I would make it, but I had my own style. I think that's what people liked. I was always doing something different, breaking the rules. Can you imagine that I got fined two pesos for not wearing stockings in the Teatro Porteño? I was in thirty movies and twenty plays, you know. I was on television too."

I watch her drift off to sleep, listening to her breathe, trying to memorize every detail of this room, the sound of her voice, the scent of her perfume. On a small dressing table with a mirror, there are photos. One is a theatrical headshot of Tita as a young dark-haired woman, her head tilted at a provocative angle, defiance all over her face. Another is a picture of a woman and two children – a boy and a girl who could be Tita as a child. Maybe Laura found her mother after all.

Beside the photos is an ornate silver hairbrush and matching hand mirror. On the floor beside the dressing table, there's an open suitcase that's half-full of clothes, a makeup bag, and some playbills, as if she's planning a trip or has just come back from one. The dressing room of a star.

I tiptoe out of the room. Nina is sitting outside in the hallway. She stands up, takes my hands between hers, and kisses me on the cheek. "Thank you for coming. Please come again if you have time. Just ask for me at reception. There is little that brings her joy now. Most of her friends are no longer with us, and there aren't many people left who she can share her memories with."

I go back the next day, but Tita is asleep. After sitting beside her bed with Nina for a while, I kiss La Bonita's forehead gently and whisper my promise that I'll never forget her.

∞

When I call Silvio's parents, his mother, Clara, picks up the phone. "Can you come on Thursday? It's the twenty-ninth. We always have *ñoquis** on the twenty-ninth of the month. It's good luck," she says in that typical *porteña* way that always provides the perfect opening for easy conversation.

"My parents still make *ñoquis* on the twenty-ninth too."

She laughs. "Good. We'll make a lot. You can tell them that you won't be hungry."

On Thursday, I take the subway to Pasco and then walk the three blocks to their place. Like every

---

* gnocchi, dumplings made of potato and flour

neighbourhood in Buenos Aires, it's packed with cars and people shopping and sitting in cafés. I press the buzzer for apartment 2B.

"*Hola*, it's me. Ale."

"Ale *querida*! *Bienvenida*!* Come in." Silvio's father, Enzo. He buzzes me in and I walk up the stairs to their apartment.

Enzo opens the door, welcoming me with a kiss on the cheek. He's not much taller than me, solidly-built, with a full head of silver hair.

Silvio's mother, Clara, is lithe, like her son, and has his smile. "Come in and sit down, *mi amor*. We can drink some *mate* before we have dinner."

Their living room is bright and airy. An open door leads out to a small balcony overlooking the street. There is a bookshelf with a small television set and a few photos – some of Silvio and one of me that Silvio took, catching me by surprise when I was first teaching him to dance.

"I've brought you something from Silvio."

Enzo holds the package for a few seconds before gently unwrapping the tissue paper around the small red-and-white glass bottle. Silvio has inherited his father's moments of measured silence. Enzo pulls out the note that's rolled up inside it. After reading it, he hands it to Clara. "Look, it's in English."

She smiles as she reads it aloud, "I made this one

---

* Welcome.

with Canadian colours. Until I see you again. Kisses, Silvio." She gives the bottle and the note back to Enzo, and he places them beside a picture of Silvio on the bookshelf. The water for *mate* is boiling. Enzo rests his hands on Clara's shoulders, pausing for a few seconds on his way to the kitchen.

While we wait for him to come back, Clara flips through a photo album and shows me pictures of Silvio kicking a soccer ball, eating ice cream, and walking to school in the white coat all Argentinian school children wear. They look like little doctors.

"We miss Silvio very much, but we're glad he's in Canada. He can build a future now," she says.

"Yes, a future," Enzo says as he comes back in. "Argentina is once again facing a financial crisis. Strikes every week. So many of our people don't have a future. Working two or three small jobs just to have enough food to eat and living with memories no one should have." He looks straight at me. "Look at Silvio's friend Santiago. He lives with his parents around the corner on Moreno. His brother, Tomás, disappeared during those terrible times."

I nod. "Yes. Silvio told me."

Clara points to a boy in one of the photos. "That's Tomás. There, beside Silvio. We were at the Botanical Gardens that day. I think he was about five then. Look at those smiles! And there's Santiago, his little brother. He used to follow Tomás around everywhere. I sometimes see him and his mother when I go shopping. He's so skinny and nervous now. He won't look you in the eyes, and he can't walk very well after that car hit him."

The ghosts have names in this house. They don't hide in whispers or slide, anonymous, into dreams.

"My grandmother disappeared. Her name is Marcela. Marcela Torres."

Enzo nods and closes his eyes.

"Yes, Silvio told us." Clara touches my cheek and gently pushes my hair away from my face, the way my mother would.

Enzo pours hot water into the *mate*. "So many of us have lost too much."

After the *mate*, we sit down to dinner in the kitchen. A plate is piled high with more *ñoquis* than can possibly be eaten by just three people. There are two framed pictures on the wall beside the small fridge – one of a young Tita Merello and a faded one of D'Arienzo conducting his tango orchestra in one of his typical poses – standing six inches away from the *bandoneón* player and staring straight into his face.

"Well, *queridas*, we've lost a lot, but at least we still have *ñoquis* and the tango and some good wine!" He smiles, stands up, and pushes play on a battered cassette player that sits on the top of the fridge.

Tita Merello's voice fills the room.

"I went to see her," I say. "Tita. At the Favaloro Foundation."

"Ah, Tita! She actually let you in?"

"Yes. She's very old now."

"Incredible! They say she won't speak to many people anymore," Clara says.

"She didn't talk much, but she sang a bit. It was the tango my grandfather says he wrote when he was a kid, and she sang it then. That was a long time ago, but I think she remembered it."

Enzo gives me that *porteño* look that means 'come on, *querida,* don't just talk about it' – palms and eyes towards the ceiling. Silvio does this to me and Lito used to as well.

Enzo turns off the cassette player. "OK, I'm serious. Put down that fork and have some wine. The *ñoquis* can wait. I want to hear this tango by your *abuelito* that you and Tita Merello sang."

I take another mouthful of wine. As I sing the first lines, my head is spinning. "*Flaco, fino, y delicado, durito muy bien parado.*"

Enzo smiles and gasps the whole way through the tango and makes me sing it again. The second time through, he records it and helps me finish it off. "*Flaco, puto, y bobina, que nacistes en la ruina. Sin un mango pa' morfar.*" His fist punches the air. "*Eso! Brava, piba!* What a tango!"

Lito's music has found its way back home.

After we've finished eating, Enzo changes the tape in the cassette player. "And now, some D'Arienzo. *Bailamos?*" He nods at me – a *cabeceo*. When I nod back and stand up, he moves the chairs aside to clear some space for us to dance to "El Flete."

Clara claps and laughs. "*Che,* Ale*!* Your *abuelito* really taught you how to dance! Have you been to any *milongas* in Buenos Aires yet?"

"Yes. El Arranque, El Beso, and Salón Canning."

Enzo slaps his thigh. "Great! Next time you and Silvio visit Argentina, we'll all go to El Arranque. It's very close. We can walk from here, straight up Pasco to Bartolomé Mitre. We always buy an ice cream and take it to the Primero de Mayo Park on the way. And now, I'm going to dance with my beautiful wife."

He nods at Clara. They look as if they're dancing even before she stands up. As they move to "El Choclo," I think of La Bonita singing it at her first audition at the Teatro Avenida and wonder what happened to the other girls who were there – Mirta and Angelina – and the people on the *estancia* – Celia the cook, Luisa, Señor González and his son, Enrique.

After dinner, Enzo runs his hand slowly over the pictures I've brought them of Silvio in his studio and the two of us in Queen's Park and on Toronto Island. He's trying not to let me see the tears in his eyes.

"Take good care of our son," Clara says as we kiss goodbye.

"And please, keep teaching him to dance tango," Enzo says, smiling. "So that he can make you look good at El Arranque."

"Or we can dance in Toronto," I say.

"Ah, that would be nice. Imagine us in Canada, Clara! We'd better start learning English."

I don't tell them Silvio's going to send them the money for the plane tickets to Toronto next year. He wants it to be a surprise.

Crossing Moreno on my way back to the subway station, I see a man half a block ahead of me. He has a ponytail and is wearing a pair of baggy jeans and a faded T-shirt, just like the young man I saw with his mother in the Plaza de Mayo. He also walks with a slight limp. I walk faster to catch up to him. As I pass, he turns to look at me. It's not the same man. There are many Santiagos out there.

∞

I stand in front of the three-storey building on Matheu in Parque Patricios, where Señora Luz' daughter, Mariana, lives in Lito's old apartment on the second floor. My parents still haven't gotten round to selling it, and they'd rather have someone living there than leave it empty. Señora Luz lives in an apartment across the street. My mother told me she lost her husband to cancer when Mariana was only five. I take a deep breath and push the buzzer marked 1A and the front door opens. They're already out on the landing in the hallway above me, hands clasped and smiling. "Come up, *mi amor*," they both say at once, excited. I start up the stairs to meet one of the last people to talk to my grandmother the day she disappeared.

Señora Luz is round and fat and wearing a black dress. Mariana, who is my mother's age, is squeezed into a low-cut pink T-shirt and leopard-print jeans. Her nails are very long and match her sparkly pink running shoes. She has bleached hair, like the older women in the *milongas*. I can't imagine my mother in anything like the outfit her old friend is wearing

One on either side of me, they hug and kiss me and usher me in. Lito's apartment is so much smaller and darker than I imagined. There's a tiny kitchen off a room that serves as both living and dining room. Not much light comes in through the single window. There's a soft old couch piled with cushions against one wall, a large wooden dining table and chairs on the opposite one, and a television in the corner that's much too big for this room. The television is on, tuned to what looks like a talk show. The sound is off.

As in Silvio's parents' apartment, there are photos, but here, they cover almost every inch of available wall space. A lot of them are of Lito and my grandmother

– on their wedding day, at the beach, walking in parks, dancing.

"My father died when I was very young and your *abuelito* was like a father to me. All the photos are here just as he left them so he can see them when he comes back," Mariana says. "Look, that's me with your mother at Palermo Lakes, Ale. We were nine. Marcela was my best friend. And there are your grandparents walking behind us. I remember it was a beautiful day. We went for pastries in a café on Juncal after our walk."

This makes me think of Lito's story of El Dentista walking his bicycle along Juncal, hoping for a glimpse of Claudia through a café window.

Mariana tells me she moved into this apartment with her daughter and son after her husband left her. "He's had three women since me. They're welcome to that miserable son of a bitch. The only good things he gave me were my two kids. My son lives with his girlfriend now. They run a newspaper kiosk in Barrio Belgrano. My daughter and her husband live in Córdoba and they're expecting a second baby, so I'll be a grandmother again soon."

Señora Luz shakes her head slowly. "I told Mariana not to marry that guy, but she didn't listen. He was bad from the start, spending all his time drinking and losing money on the *burros*. She never listens to me. And just look at that outfit she's wearing!"

"OK, Mami. Enough! I'll wear what I want."

I can't help thinking of Dolores and Gloria.

Señora Luz looks straight at me, her eyes shining with tears. "Your *abuelita* was an angel, Ale! I should have gone shopping with her that day she disappeared. Maybe if we'd been together, those men wouldn't have taken her."

"Please, Mami, don't start. It only makes you cry. I've told you so many times that wouldn't have stopped them. They would have just taken both of you."

Señora Luz pulls a lace handkerchief from her sleeve and dabs at her eyes.

After empanadas and salad followed by tea and pastries, it's already nine o'clock, and Mariana insists I stay the night, so I call Gabriela to tell her I'll be back tomorrow. I sleep in what used to be my mother's bed in a narrow room with a window onto the street, the room where she would drift off to sleep to the sound of tango from Lito's radio in the next room. There's another picture of Lito and my grandmother on the bedside table. Her name was Marcela, but what would I have called her? Even in my dreams, she has only ever been a ghost, a part of the stories Lito told me, but nameless, almost formless. I have to give her a name, my *abuelita*.

I will have to go out and look for you myself, Lita. There's another walk I need to take tomorrow.

The next day, I walk along Rondeau towards

Pichincha. A short distance from where my grandmother was last seen is the old Caseros prison. It's not used anymore. The flesh-coloured walls have crumbled away in places, leaving rust-grey patches that look like wounds. A few branches have sprouted from cracks. Looming behind it is the newer extension of the prison, also due to be demolished. The prison that Videla built.

I walk back to Matheu and then down to Caseros. The streets are busy, as they are everywhere in Buenos Aires. People doing everyday things – buying tonight's dinner, drinking coffee in cafés, greeting neighbours, going to work. Just a normal morning. It's hard to imagine that things were once so different here – lives and dreams shattered, families brutally torn apart. I search the faces of people I pass on the street, again not sure what I was hoping to find here. My feet are on the same pavement as my grandmother's were when she went shopping for the last time, but I can't feel her here. Once more, I'm scrambling for connection. I stop, not knowing which way to go next.

A woman smiles and asks me if I'm lost. I want to say yes, I'm completely lost, but no map will help me. Instead, I smile back and say, "No, I'm fine." But I'm not. I suddenly need Lito.

Along Caseros, left at Lavardén, and down to the corner of Uspallata. Las Tres Violetas.* Lito told me

---

* The Three Violets

that he and my *abuelita* used to go to that café. A chalkboard outside lists the daily specials – *matambre caseros, jamón serrano, colita de cuadril, pastel de papas.* I take a deep breath, push the door open, and feel as if I've gone back in time. The walls are covered with the same white ceramic tiles as the counter and hung with a collection of random objects that look as though they've been added as acquired over the years with no thought of what should go where. A Réal Madrid soccer plaque, an antique clock, a couple of small, faded landscape paintings, a religious poster, a small mirror, a shelf lined with bottles. An antique espresso machine takes up half the counter.

The place is empty except for a waiter, wearing a white shirt and black suit pants, and an elderly couple, who are sitting side by side at two wooden tables that have been pushed together. There's a half-empty bottle of soda water and an assortment of glasses and plates in front of them. The man has his arms crossed and is leaning back in his chair. The woman is leaning forward, both arms on the table. They eye me as I enter.

"*Buenos días*," they say together and nod.

"*Buenos días.*" I nod back and smile.

Lito was always proud of his *matambre,* a meat roll stuffed with egg. I sit down and order that and a *café con leche.* The waiter looks about seventy. I take a deep breath. "My grandfather is Tito. Alberto Torres. Do you remember him? He used to work in the hardware store on Caseros."

Silence. Then the faces light up and I'm suddenly in the middle of three embraces, everybody talking at once.

"Tito's granddaughter! For the love of God!"

"Remember when he used to bring his wife and daughter here?"

"Yes, I remember. Tito and Marcelita!"

"Their daughter's name was Marcelita too."

"You look just like your mother, *piba*. She is very pretty."

"What dancers your grandparents were!"

"I remember them in the *milonga* at Club Huracán."

They're careful not to say too much about my grandmother, and I'm careful not to tell them that Lito is slipping into a place in a song that he and I used to sing. "En el País de Nomeacuerdo." In the Land of I Don't Remember.

∞

The Thursday before I leave Buenos Aires, I go back to the Plaza de Mayo. I hug the women at the book table and tell them I'm returning to Canada but I'll come and see them next time. Again, I join *Las Madres* as they circle the plaza. Then I see her just ahead of me – the woman I thought might be Santiago's mother.

The same brown skirt and scuffed brown shoes. I can tell she's seen me too. She slows down to let me catch up to her and then takes my hand and holds onto it tightly.

"You are Silvio's friend?"

"Yes. I'm Alejandra. Ale."

"I'm Milena, the mother of Tomás and Santiago. I'm sorry I didn't speak to you the other day. My son Santiago, he doesn't really like…to talk to people, but he's a good boy. Well, I hope you understand. He had an accident…a car…"

"It's OK, señora. I understand."

"Silvio told you?"

"Yes."

"My son is over there, waiting for me." She nods in the direction of a bench on the other side of the plaza. Santiago has a cigarette in one hand and a large bottle of a bright-orange drink in the other.

Milena and I walk arm in arm in silence for about ten more minutes until the group begins to disperse, and then she guides me towards Santiago. He's wearing the same pair of baggy jeans and the green T-shirt with the ripped sleeve. As we approach, he stands up.

"Santiago, this is Alejandra, Silvio's friend. All the way from Canada!"

"*Hola.*" Santiago gives me the traditional greeting – a perfunctory kiss on the cheek. He shifts from one foot to the other and tugs at his ponytail.

"Santiago, it's good to finally meet you. Silvio has told me about you."

"Oh?"

"Yes." I'm not sure what to say to him. I wish Silvio were here. He shoves his hands in his pockets and stares at the ground.

Milena unpins the photo that's attached to her shirt. "This is a photo of my son Tomás."

In the picture is a boy of about fifteen with a guitar hanging from a strap across his chest. He's smiling directly into the camera. When I try to give it back to her, she shakes her head and clasps my hand. "No, please keep it. It's for Silvio and you, so that you'll remember my son."

"Silvio told me about Tomás. He will always remember him," I say. I want to give them something. All I can think of is to dig in my bag for my notebook, remove a page, and scribble down my name, address, and phone number in Canada. "Silvio has your address. Is it OK if we write to you?"

"Yes, yes. It's OK."

Then I remember the photos of Lita in my wallet, the ones that Señora Luz gave me. I hesitate for a few seconds before I take one out and slip it into Milena's hand. "She's my grandmother. Her name is Marcela Torres. She disappeared."

Santiago shudders. Milena closes her eyes, takes a deep breath, and puts her arms around me.

"She is beautiful, your *abuelita*,"

We hold onto each other in silence, unable to summon any words. Behind her, I can see Santiago, looking down at the ground and raking his fingers over the top of his head. As they're leaving, he takes his mother's arm.

"Please say thank you to Silvio for his letters. I read them." he says.

I watch them walk away. Milena looks back at me one last time, smiles, and waves. I have no idea where to put myself, so I walk to the bench and sit where Santiago had been. I will my hands to stop shaking and stare at the picture Milena has entrusted me with. Tomás – one more star in the night sky.

More than sixty years after you, Lito, as I trace your walk along Corrientes, your footsteps echo. *Corrientes*, currents. I think about rivers after all and how they flow into one another. I think of La Rusa and the secrets carried by our little river in Canada that made their way into my dreams.

From a second-floor window, tango drifts over bright-red flowers hanging in a balcony – Carlos Gardel singing "Volver," return. I have returned to a place I've never been, except when we danced in the kitchen, Gardel's voice winding through scratches on the tango records you'd brought to Canada.

As I get closer to the place you told me you saw my

abuelita in her orange tango dress, I imagine riding up to the second floor in the shaky birdcage elevator and standing outside the door to the room where it's always evening. I imagine the piano, the red velvet curtains, and the music from the phonograph. But when I arrive at 348 Corrientes, I find a door to a parking garage for what look like offices above. Shaking inside, I choke back tears. If stories are not told, they disappear.

In Buenos Aires, I sometimes feel I'm drifting in and out of dreams with no border between waking and sleep or truth and myth, just as it was in Lito's stories. I've discovered that some of his details were rearranged, some embellished, even invented, infused with stories told in tangos. 348 Corrientes is in the first line of the lyrics to "A Media Luz." But, as in all memories, the inventions that fill the gaps sometimes hold the truth, the essence. Lito gave me a city filled with legends, whose background music was tango. And in all legends, suffering is transformed into something exquisite, something that sustains us.

The memories he distilled for me, which shaped me and have brought me here, are in my blood. They were in the air I breathed, mixed into the *masa** for the *medialunas*, stirred into my *chocolate*. Every cell in my body has absorbed them and I'm powerless to do anything but submit. I do not have the choice of living

---

* dough

without them. I will also continue to fill the spaces in the stories and they'll become my own.

I believe I've found La Bonita, but I'll always wonder what happened to the others – Doña Pepa, El Ciego, El Dentista, Armando, El Loco, La Rusa and her kids, Los Palitos, Manuel and his little brothers and father, Juan, and the other people in the house that Lito never told me about. And there will be times when I wonder if they really even existed at all.

Silvio was right. The rooms in the house are not numbered and Lito's numbers don't make sense. I'm not even sure if the house I've found is really the one he grew up in. But it doesn't matter if the numbers were real or if the house exists in brick and stone. He never told me the exact address, but he gave me the internal map to find it whenever I need to be there. Just listen to the music and your feet will move by themselves. Lito's stories and music are the mortar that will always hold it together.

In my room overlooking Balcarce Street, I place Silvio's blue bottle filled with Expósito's words on the windowsill and slip the lottery tickets under it. Beside it, I put the paper flower from the little girl in Retiro and Doña Pepa's piece of star. My amulets.

My dress is hanging on the back of the chair, ready for the *milonga* later tonight. I try on my new shoes and, three inches taller, walk carefully out to the balcony. It's a clear night filled with stars. From the café down the street comes the hum of conversation, the clink of glasses, and the insistent wail of the *bandoneón*.

I close my eyes and breathe in the night and my feet start to move. I'm doing the only thing I can – dancing with La Renga, with all of them. Part of the tango. Part of the story.

I came to Argentina to keep a promise to you, Lito, but I have learned that this journey is also for me because, just at the moment between waking and sleep – *a media luz* – I leave the outsider on one side of the silver river and float across on the shadow of a dream to where everything you told me is real, and they are all there, waiting for me.

∞

Silvio meets me at the airport when I return to Toronto. In the taxi, my stories tumble out, colliding and running over one another as I lead him through the streets of Buenos Aires. Up and down the stairs and from room to room in Lito's house. Into Tita's room, where she and I sang Lito's tango. I tell him how I danced under the stars in the Plaza Dorrego and ate *matambre* in Las Tres Violetas, where everyone remembered Lito and my *abuelita*.

At home, I empty out my suitcase on the floor, pulling out the book I bought from *Las Madres*, volumes of tango lyrics and Clemente comics from a bookshop on Corrientes, my tango shoes, a letter from Silvio's parents with a new tango tape, postcards, a box of *alfajores,* some *mate* for Lito, a poster of a young Tita Merello from a shop in San Telmo, the paper flower I got from the little girl outside the train station. I have so many stories and I want to tell him all of them.

"And I have this." I give him the photo from Milena. "I saw Santiago and his mother in the Plaza de Mayo."

"Tomás." He turns the photo over and over in his hands.

"Santiago got your letters. He said to thank you and he—"

He puts his finger to his lips, kisses me on the forehead, and stands up. He opens the envelope from his father and slides the new tape into the cassette player. Fresedo's orchestra. "Volver."

"OK, *piba*, put on those new tango shoes and let's dance," he says.

I close my eyes and settle into his embrace. "I forgot to tell you I bought some *quiniela* tickets. I used the numbers of the rooms. We didn't win."

"I think we did," he says.

∞

The phone rings on a sunny morning in September. My mother's voice sounds very far away and I know she's been crying.

"Ale, the doctor has just been here. Lito is slipping away. I think you should come."

Silvio and I drive to Peterborough in silence. When we arrive at my parents' house, I can't get out of the car fast enough. I race up the stairs to Lito's bedroom. My parents and Carlita are with him. Tango music is playing on his cassette player, and he looks as if he's sleeping. I kiss him and tell him I love him over and over again. I bury my face in his pillow. For hours, I sing to him and tell him stories. After the story of how La Bonita and I sang his tango in Buenos Aires, he leaves us.

"He was waiting for you," my father says.

∞

Lito will never meet our daughter who'll be born in a few months, but she will know him. We'll sing his tangos and look up at the night sky to find his star. We'll go down to Kensington Market and eat empanadas. She and Silvio will draw El Dentista's bicycle and El Loco's hat covered with stars. In Buenos Aires, we'll all sit under the big tree in the middle of the patio. Together, we'll go up the stairs and count them the way Esteban did. We'll drink *chocolate* and eat *medialunas* in the Café Tortoni. We'll sit beside the little river near my parents' house and listen for secrets.

We'll tell her why we called her Laura. And when she's old enough, she'll read Lito's stories – my stories – and they'll become hers too.

And we'll dance.

At Half-Light

EPILOGUE

In 1996, Adolfo Scilingo, a former Argentinian naval officer who had been assigned to ESMA, broke the military pact of silence and publicly confessed to the journalist Horacio Verbitsky that he had assisted in "death flights," in which naked prisoners, sedated with injections of sodium pentothal, were dropped into the Río de la Plata from planes or helicopters. The prisoners had been told they were just being transferred and the injections were vaccines.

In April 2005, a Spanish court sentence found Scilingo guilty of crimes against humanity, including torture, unlawful detention, and thirty counts of murder. He is serving a thirty-year sentence in a Spanish prison.

∞

In 2005, the Argentine Forensic Anthropology Team announced the identification, through DNA testing, of the remains of three of the founding Mothers of the Plaza de Mayo – Azucena Villaflor de Vicenti, María Eugenia Ponce de Bianco, and Esther Ballestrino de Careaga – as well as those of the French nun, Léonie Duquet. The bodies, with fractures indicating a fall from a great height, had washed up on the beach in December 1977 near the town of Santa Teresita, about four hundred kilometres south of the city of Buenos Aires. They had been fingerprinted and buried in anonymous mass graves in the General Lavalle municipal cemetery.

On December 8, 2005, twenty-eight years after Azucena disappeared, her ashes were buried at the foot of the May Pyramid in the centre of the Plaza de Mayo. Her surviving children had chosen the place. *Azucena* means lily. A bronze lily and plaque have been installed there.

It is estimated that five hundred children were stolen during the military dictatorship in Argentina. By 2021, as a result of the work of *Las Abuelas*, the Grandmothers of the Plaza de Mayo, one hundred and thirty of these children had been identified. They are now struggling with the knowledge that the people they had thought were their parents may have known about and, in some cases, even participated in, the disappearance, torture, and killing of their biological parents.

∞

In March 1990, Alfredo Astiz, the "Blond Angel of Death," who had betrayed the Mothers of the Plaza de Mayo, was sentenced *in absentia* by a French court to life in prison for participating in the torture and disappearance of two French nuns, Léonie Duquet and Alice Domon.

For years, Astiz was protected in Argentina by the 1986-87 pardon laws, which gave amnesty to military officers. In 2005, the pardons were revoked. Astiz and seventeen others associated with the ESMA detention centre were charged with the kidnapping, torture, and murder of eighty-six victims.

In October 2011, Astiz received a life sentence. He showed no remorse and said he would never apologize.

∞

In April 2007, General Jorge Videla's pardon for numerous homicides, kidnappings, and torture was revoked. In July 2010, he was tried on new charges of human rights violations and the deaths of thirty-one prisoners during his time in power. Videla offered no apology. During the trial, he said his intention had been to prevent a Marxist regime from being established in Argentina. In December 2010, he was sentenced to life in a civilian prison.

In July 2012, Videla received a fifty-year sentence for his participation in stealing babies from prisoners during the dictatorship. He died on May 17, 2013, five days after a fall in the shower in the Marcos Paz civilian prison. In accordance with a 2009 ruling, he was not eligible for a military funeral.

∞

Tita Merello died in the Favaloro Foundation on Christmas Eve of 2002 at the age of ninety-eight. A huge crowd and a military band were at her burial in the Chacarita Cemetery, where Carlos Gardel, Juan D'Arienzo, Ángel Villoldo, and many other icons of tango are buried.

ACKNOWLEDGEMENTS

Thanks to Miguel Libedinsky and Gwyneth Storr for their encouragement, careful reading of the manuscript, and keeping me on track with their insightful comments.

Many thanks to my editor, Marion Wyse, for her support, keen eye for detail, and the time and energy she has spent helping to bring this story to life.

Gratitude to the tango composers, lyricists, musicians, and dancers who have kept tango and its stories alive. And to *Las Madres* and *Las Abuelas*, who have never given up the search for their lost children and grandchildren.

ABOUT THE AUTHOR

Linda Walsh, originally from London, England, grew up in Canada. She is a visual artist and tango instructor and has made several trips to Buenos Aires to study tango music and dance. She has won the Commonwealth Short Story Competition for Canada and Europe and the Eden Mills Fringe Literary Contest. She has been shortlisted for the Guernica Prize and the Alice Munro Short Story Competition and longlisted for the CBC Short Story Prize. *At Half-Light* is her first novel. She lives in Toronto.

Author photograph by Daniel Walsh

Manufactured by Amazon.ca
Bolton, ON